PRETTY THUGS 5

SA'ID SALAAM

URBAN AESOP PUBLICATIONS

CHECK OUT PRETTY THUG MERCHANDISE

https://www.prettythugs.net/

DEDICATION

Dedicated to Najima Miskeena. From Allah we come, to Allah we return. Ameen.

"This nigga really is slow!" Zenobia laughed at the comical scene outside the window. She quickly went live to capture the action.

The corner exploded in an instant. One kid grabbed the cash but he was quickly grabbed by two other youths. They fought over the cash while others went for the jewels. Pretty Boy tried to fight but only had two hands. He did have a gun in his back and went for it.

"Back up!" Pretty Boy demanded and waved the gun. It got snatched as soon as he pulled it out.

The teen who grabbed the gun quickly pumped a couple bullets into his torso. The robbers dragged him a few feet trying to snatch the thick chains from his neck. One kid braced his foot against Pretty Boy's head to pull the chain off. Two different robbers ran off with one each of his custom Jordan's. They were going to have to work together to sell them .

The youths worked with the ferocity of a pack of piranhas and stripped him down to his boxers and wife beater. There was only one thing left to take so the kid with the gun stepped back up and fired a bullet into his brain. He turned and saw a shocked Zenobia holding the camera. A million viewers saw when he raised the gun again and fired. It was pointed directed at the camera when it flashed and everything went dark.

"Z!" Callie screamed since she had been watching the live. It was how she kept tabs on her friend. Lately she saw Zenobia more on social media than in real life.

"What's wrong!" Penny shouted frantically when she heard the stark terror in her voice. She was too busy with her own legions of fans to watch Zenobia's live. Callie scrambled out the door and she was hot on her heels.

"Oh my God! Oh my God!" Jovita repeated as she rushed from her room. She had her gun in her hand since she forgot her purse. Dominique burst from her room as well and joined them as they rushed to the elevator.

"Where is she!" Dominique demanded but no one had an answer. Penny still had questions though. She too got the notification when Zenobia went live and tuned in to check on her and saw the horror unfold.

"Will someone please tell me what's going on!" she pleaded and began to cry. No one could bring themselves to say what they saw so she would have to stay in the dark.

"Aaagh!" a woman gasped when the elevator door opened and saw the gun in Jovita's hand.

"It's fine. Put that away!" Dominique said to the woman and Jovita. Callie tried Zenobia's phone again but it was off.

"We don't even know where we're going!" Jovita moaned when they filed out into the lobby.

"I sure don't!" Penny griped since she still didn't know what was going on. The looks on the faces of the other guests sure seemed like they knew. She looked up at the TV over the bar and saw the headlines, a rapper shot in West Garfield park.

"I'll drive so you can shoot!" Dominique declared as they made it out to their rental car. She put the location into the GPS and pulled away from the hotel. Cousin Vinny and the groupies all piled out of the next elevator and tore out of the hotel as well. It was way too many to fit in the second rental but they would have to figure that part out on their own.

The women didn't have an exact address in the Chicago neighborhood but they wouldn't need one. The news traveled at the speed of social media so throngs of lookie-loos were enroute already. Penny's phone went crazy with condolences since the reports of a rapper dead flooded the timelines.

"What rapper! Not Z-money! Fuck naw!" Penny growled from the back seat. Again, no one answered, since no one knew.

"There!" Jovita pointed to the corner full of police activity. They got as close as they could and hopped out of the car. It was deja vu when they hopped over crime scene tape and saw a body under a bloody sheet.

"Z!" Callie shouted down at the corpse. A cop grabbed her to prevent her from pulling the sheet back.

"Over here girl," Zenobia called in between pulls on a menthol. She sat on the bumper of an ambulance to be checked out. She had been fine until Penny ran over and tackled her to the ground. She had been unscathed but now scraped her elbow on the rough Chicago street.

"Girl what happened!" Penny demanded as they were both helped up. She noticed the girl smelled like freshly smoked weed.

"Guuuuurl, this fool Pretty Boy calls himself riding around the city. I told him not to stop but he wanted to meet the people. He did and they robbed his ass," Zenobia said and shook her head. Jovita and Dominique looked at each other and went back to Zenobia. She had been in a total state of shock when Young Vaughn was killed. Now she was as casual as if they were ordering some food. "Y'all ate? I'm hungry."

"Uh, I saw the live! It looked like he shot you!" Callie fussed as she looked her over.

"That boy really tried to shoot me in my face!" she recalled without a trace of the fear that should accompany that revelation. She held up her shattered phone just to show how close that first shot came to stretching her out next to Pretty Boy. She ducked that shot and the second one went right through the double R on the headrest instead of her face.

"So, you just stayed here?" Jovita asked incredulously.

"Yeah. I smoked some weed with Nita 'ndem until the cops came," she shrugged.

"And who the fuck is Nita 'ndem?" Callie wanted to know.

"My new Chicago homies," Zenobia laughed and nodded towards a pack of girls behind the police tape. Not only did they look out for her but one of their baby daddies sold coke and ran to get some. It was a little callous but they did come all this way for drugs. She didn't want his death to be in vain.

"Let me go get their names. Ain't nobody named, 'ndem..." Dominique grumbled as she made her way over to the girls. She took each one's name so she could make sure they got free entry to tomorrow night's concerts. If they had one that is since the headliner was dead.

Cousin Vinny had just arrived to pick up the pieces of his cousin. This was the end of the road for the both of them.

CHAPTER 1

"He just hit," Jovita announced over breakfast. They had been anxiously awaiting news from the promoter to see if they could book a headliner so the show would go on.

"Shit if they cancel we can just join Doobie Daddie's tour!" Dominique said hopefully since he was the hottest rapper on the planet.

"Yeah," Penny agreed since they spoke often via text. They would probably never hook up again since she felt so guilty, but they remained friends. Plus their song was still on top of the charts.

"Shit, we need to headline this bitch! We are the Pretty Thugs!" Zenobia declared triumphantly. She wasn't even high yet so that came from the heart.

"Shit, we could!" Callie cosigned. Tours generated millions of dollars but the label didn't have it to spend when they went out. They did now since the record was selling so well. Plus the girls would definitely invest in themselves and double up.

"I guess we'll see in a few," Jovita sighed. The promoter requested an audience but she was going to finish her food first.

"Any way you girls can just chill while we're gone?" Dominique wondered as they polished off their breakfast.

"You mean like, stay in the room?" Callie asked. Penny added, "Like stay out of trouble you mean?"

"Yes! That's exactly what she means!" Jovita fussed. "For the woman who put her career over having children I still ended up with some bad ass 'chillen!"

"Girl moms for real!" Dominique echoed the sentiment, then pleaded, "Please stay out of trouble."

"Not a chance!" Callie laughed. "We put the ugg in thugs!"

"Girl we finna hit the Magnificent Mile and shop!" Zenobia cheered.

"Don't worry, we won't turn the city out," Callie laughed some more.

"What's the worst that can happen..." Penny asked but no one wanted to answer that question. So much had happened, no one wanted to see what was the worst that could happen.

The camera crew accompanied the girls on their shopping trip while Jovita and Dominique went to meet the promoter. They drove over to a local radio station where he did an interview on Pretty Boy's demise. He left out the Key man life insurance policy he had on the high risk rapper. It would make the untimely demise profitable.

"Hey," the man said and sighed like he had more bad news. Both women were prepared for it and already starting thinking about plan B. They may not be able to get the big arenas like he could but would press on without him.

"Hey," they both replied, and tilted their heads like a dare. None of the five women really realized how much they were becoming alike. They had all rubbed off on each other for both the better and worse.

"Crazy night! I'm just glad Z-money didn't get harmed," he said.

"I wouldn't say that, but thanks," Jovita said while Dominique cosigned with a, "Yeah."

"Well, based on the numbers, I think we can just add another opening act. Two maybe and press on," he stuttered and stammered like even he knew it was some bullshit. "We can just slide the Pretty Thugs into the headliner spot and finish the rest of the dates."

"Sounds good!" Jovita cheered to his delight while Dominique donned a 'what the fuck are you talmbout' look on her face. She almost spoke up but Jovita wasn't quite finished. "Except, hell naw! Not for the same bread!"

"Word! So we take up the slack while you keep the change?" Dominique snipped and rolled her eyes.

"Huh? Naw, I, we, see..." the man scrambled since that's exactly what he planned to do. "We would renegotiate of course!"

"Nothing to negotiate. You'll either pay the group five million to finish the tour or you won't," Jovita said and shrugged like it was as simple as that. Only because it was. Dominique was still nice enough to expound.

"Can you rap?" Dominique asked with a laugh. "Cuz you'll have to headline your damn self!"

"I can do two million, but..." he sighed and laid it out.

There was an offer on the table that would definitely support spending the money. Would they go for it or not was the question.

"WE MADE IT BACK!" Callie announced when they met their managers for dinner.

"Yup. No police cars! No helicopters," Penny added.

"No fire trucks either, Left Eye," Dominique cracked.

"No running across the roulette table and kicking hoes in the face either!" Zenobia snickered as she got in on the action. It was pretty funny, plus she was high.

"It was a poker table, thank you very much," Penny huffed in her own defense.

"So, anyway," Jovita said when she could slide in. She lost the coin toss so this one was on her. "We met with the promoter today."

"And..." the group sang like a singing group.

"They offered two million to take over the tour and..." was as far as she got before having to wait for the celebration to die down. There was even more money on the table but she didn't get that far.

Dominique just shook her head at what she knew was coming. She had made her point clear when she offered to stick the point of her umbrella up the man's ass. It wasn't her decision to make and her client stood to make a lot of money.

"What?" Zenobia asked when she noticed the stoic looks on their faces.

"Did I mention they offered ten million to headline the tour for the next album?" Jovita asked and raised her eyebrows. All she got was skeptical titled heads and twisted lips. "Plus attendance incentives!"

"What's the catch yo?" Zenobia asked, sounding like Callie. "You always said no one gives up nothing for nothing..."

"It's always something," Callie finished the teaching Jovita taught with every deal. It was true so she negotiated the best deals she could for her girls.

"Well, they want the fake Pretty Thugs to open for you guys," she sighed and braced herself. Dominique's reaction was bad so she expected worse.

"Man, I know you ain't even say what I know you just didn't just say!" Callie said and confused herself. "I mean you just said..."

"So we supposed to perform with the same bitches who stole our name, be dissing us all over social media and cut my girl face?" Zenobia dared.

"Not perform with. They will open and leave. You'll be the stars of the show. Separate hotels. You get the jet and the penthouse suites," Jovita replied and looked to Dominique for help.

"Tuh!" was all she had coming from the new vice president.

"Oh, and they made a diss track too!" Callie snitched to Zenobia who hadn't heard it.

"Which we got Mike to shelve if they want to get on the tour," Dominique spoke up. That was one thing she did agree with even without the couple hundred grand she would make from the tour.

"We should do it," Penny smiled like she had a bright idea.

"We should?" Callie and Zenobia shot back.

"Hells yeah! What better way to show the real from the fake than on the same stage!" she suggested. "Them hoes is lipstick on a pig with lyrics someone else wrote for them! We are the real deal!"

"She does have a point," Dominique chimed in again. "But, Ion think we should commit to the second tour? Not yet."

"I agree. It's worth more than he's offering," Jovita concluded. Not to mention how much it would be worth if they sponsored the tour themselves.

"So, we are contributing to the bum bitches of America scholarship fund?" Callie sighed. Asking was her tacit approval.

"We doing it!" Dominique announced. It was too late for tonight's show but they would catch the next stop in the next city.

"YO Z?" a voice called as the Thugs came out of their dressing room. A few local acts had paid the promoter to fill the void left when they got moved to the headline.

"Hey Cousin Vinny," Zenobia sang and rushed over to hug his neck. This was the first time she saw him since the murder the night before. "How you holding up?"

"Not good man. Can you fall through the suite after your set?" he asked woefully.

"Man..." she began to decline since she wasn't in the mood for all those folks. She had a nice little stash of drugs she could use on her own. Then the thought of having to sneak hits in the bathroom with the water running came to mind. Then the discriminatory glances of her friends when she came out with the cocaine sniffles. "Yeah, for a sec."

"Cool. I'll see you then," Vinny sighed and turned away. The remorse was real since he lost both his family and his gravy train. He was set for life since he controlled all of Pretty Boy's assets, royalties and insurance policy. He actually jumped in the air and clicked his heels when the man was murdered. Not that he wanted him dead, the insurance just didn't cover the drug overdose that was in his future.

"What he want?" Callie demanded when Zenobia returned.

"To talk about his cousin. I'ma holla at him after we wreck this stage!" she said and hyped herself up. They all shed their normal personas when their music began booming through the arena. This was their first headline so they ran out and gave Chi-town their money's worth.

P-money once again proved she was a star when she ran out into the crowd. The adoring fans held her in midair while she rapped and danced, then placed her back safely on the stage. There would be a few up the skirt videos floating around the next day. The pink P-money panties would go viral and sell millions.

"Y'all did that!" Dominique declared when the sweaty Thugs ran off the stage. "Now, let's eat!"

"Thug shit!" P-money shouted. It always took longer to come back for her since P-money and Penny were so far apart.

"That was Crazy!" Callie huffed. They just rocked a whole arena as the headliners. It was their names in lights and she loved it.

"Whew! Let's get back to the hotel!" Zenobia suggested. She did want to shower and change out of the wet clothes but she had an ulterior motive. She wanted to get high.

"Yeah. I guess we can eat at the hotel," Dominique shrugged. It didn't matter as long as they ate.

"Y'ALL GO 'HEAD. I'll meet y'all down there," Zenobia said after showering and pulling on a sweat suit with Pretty Thugs on the ass. It was hard to read with all that ass jiggling but it was a good seller.

"Mmhm," Callie and Penny hummed together. They heard that song before and knew how it ended. There were times they wouldn't see her until they reached the next city. Zenobia started to fuss but decided to go get high instead.

"These bitches be acting like they my mama. My mamdead," she grumbled and griped as she marched down the hall. She was always a little salty when sober. The thought crossed her mind to take a bump in the elevator but it was occupied when it arrived. A snooty black lady clutched her purse and leaned into her husband when she got on. "Bitch please!"

After the awkward ride down to the lobby she got access to the penthouse elevator. She almost took a bump then but remembered cameras were everywhere these days. She let out a frustrated groan and watched the numbers roll by on the display. Finally it opened into the empty penthouse.

"Hey," Cousin Vinny greeted. He was in a good mood but rocked a sourpuss face since he was supposed to be in mourning and all.

"Where's everyone at?" she wondered since it was usually a full blown party going on.

"Sent they asses home. The party's over," he explained. Not just because Pretty Boy was dead but he wasn't wasting his money on keeping all those folks high.

"Well, I got my own coke!" she said and dumped some out on the coffee table. Vinny looked down her shirt when she leaned over to inhale the lines she made.

"Here," he offered and handed her a flute of champagne.

"Thanks?" she asked since he sat right up next to her. It was odd but he was in mourning so she let it slide. Little did she know he took that as acquiescence so he put a hand on her thigh. She looked down at it, then up at him. "Umm?"

"We're finally alone," he said and leaned in for a kiss. Zenobia was so confused she just sat there. Didn't participate nor resist. Again, he took it as acquiescence and went further by trying to lay her down.

"Un-uh! What the fuck is you doing?" she fussed and resisted laying on her back.

"Come on now! You know you want this," he moaned and puckered for another kiss.

"You tripping!" she shot back and struggled to get away. It took all she had since he wasn't taking 'no' for an answer. She got really scared and screamed "Stop!"

"You tripping!" Vinny spat and loosened his grip. "You ain't say shit last time you let me hit."

"Last time? When I let you hit? I ain't never even fuck your limp dick cousin!" she shouted and stood. "Fuck is you 'talmbout, let you hit last time?"

"Nothing," he relented and left her alone. He had taken so much inebriated and incapacitated pussy he confused it with his consenting conquest. He raised his hands and let her leave.

"These niggas be delusional as fuck!" Zenobia shouted. She was so flustered by the episode she needed another bump and took one as the elevator rode down to the lobby. She made it a double before heading over to the restaurant and finding her friends.

"What's wrong with you?" Penny demanded when she sat down.

"Huh?" Zenobia asked and pawed at her nose to make sure she didn't leave any residue.

"Nothing," Penny said and shook her head. Dominique couldn't ignore it anymore but decided it could wait until they reached Cleveland.

CHAPTER 2

"**N**ow this is what the fuck I'm talmbout!" Callie grunted when they boarded the private jet once used by Pretty Boy. He was dead now, so he wouldn't need it.

"Get used to it," Jovita reminded once again since Callie was the least accepting of her new status. It was like she was ready for someone to shake her awake from this wonderful dream.

"Oh, I am!" Zenobia cheered. She had popped a perc and snorted the last of her coke so had a nice buzz going. The plane hadn't even taken off, yet but she was already at cruising altitude.

"Been used to it!" Penny stated. She didn't mean to brag but it felt good to return to the status she once knew. Callie couldn't read minds so she rolled her eyes at what she heard.

"Look, we need to talk..." Dominique said once they were all seated. It was time to have the same talk mothers all over the world have with their children before they go somewhere new. The standard don't touch anything or no one. "Just stay away from them rats. They have nothing to lose and everything to gain by beefing with you."

"She's right. They need this way more than you guys. We're here for the check. They need the exposure," Jovita added.

"Shit, I'm good," Callie responded quickly. A little too quickly and turned all heads in her direction. "Bruh, I'm collecting mils like them hoes collect STDs."

"She good then," Dominique agreed since the money was pouring in.

"I'm good too," Penny replied since her personal stock was rising faster than the whole group. They were all stars but she was a superstar. Legions of little white girls wanted to be P-money.

Jovita was working with a company to make a P-money make up kit. Another was developing a P-money Halloween costume. Her jersey sold the most out of the Pretty Thug jerseys. Closely followed by C-money, while Z-money brought up the rear.

Everyone looked over to Zenobia for her reply but she wasn't with them. She was physically on the plane but had scrolled ahead to Cleveland on her phone. She had run out of pills and coke and that was more important than whatever they were talking about. She felt all the eyes on her and the cabin go silent.

"What?" she asked when she looked up and saw everyone looking at her.

"We were just making sure you guys are OK with those girls on the roster?" Jovita asked politely.

"Ion care," Zenobia shrugged and went back to her search. She found a few pain management centers, but those required prescriptions. She let out a sigh and kept on scrolling.

"That's settled then," Dominique declared and leaned back to enjoy the private jet.

Penny went back to her followers while Callie and her new boo texted back and forth. Both eagerly anticipated her return to the city so they could spend some time together. Plus she wanted to fuck him.

"LADIES!" the promoter cheered when the limo arrived at the hotel. Bumping them to the headliner spot was paying off already. A second show had been added, plus they were getting requests from Idaho and Iowa. Places they had never been before, but thanks to P-money now could.

Not to mention their rider was a third of what Pretty Boy was requesting. He didn't have to rent a Rolls Royce for them to drive in every spot. Especially since the one from Chicago had been sold four times before it was found stripped.

"How was the flight?" he asked even though he already knew since he always flew private himself.

"Everything was as expected," Jovita answered quickly. She wanted to make sure he knew it was their act that made it possible. He wasn't doing them any favors by giving them what they deserved. They all boarded the elevator up to the penthouse level.

"I'm sure you'll find the accommodations up to par as

well. I'm down the hall if you need me," he said and headed down the hall.

"This is dope!" Callie admitted when they entered the spectacular suite. They spread out to look around but Zenobia eased back out the door. She headed right down the same hall and tapped on the door.

"Come in! Just put them by the door," he called, assuming it was the bellhop with his bags.

"Put what by the door?" Zenobia asked, since she wasn't the bellhop and didn't carry bags.

"Oh, I thought... Anyway, what can I help you with?" he asked even though he had a clue since she had been hanging out with Pretty Boy for most of the tour.

"I know you got our rider but, I have a few personal requests," she said and lifted her chin like it was her right. She was part of the hottest group in the country now that the Money Dance was officially the number one song in the land.

"Hard or soft?" he asked, hoping she would say soft. Cocaine is one hell of a drug but there are still levels to that shit. Even though the only difference between coke and crack was just a matter of time.

"Ewww!" Zenobia grimaced at the thought of smoking crack. She had awakened a few times to see Pretty Boy pulling off the pipe like a hooker sucking a dick.

"Soft it is," he nodded. "Anything else?"

"Perc, or Oxy," she added since she had a routine. A dangerous routine that teetered on a precipice of destruction.

"Gotcha. Give me a few," he said and pulled out his phone. Zenobia headed out while he made a few calls. He was plugged into every city on the tour so drugs were on the way by the time she eased back into their suite.

"This is fiyah!" Zenobia squealed as she rejoined the tour before she was even missed. They weren't the only ones checking out their new accommodations since the fake Prety Thugs had arrived in town as well. They flew in but would join the bus of other opening acts and support personnel.

"THIS IS LIT!" white girl Ki-ki exclaimed as she looked around the double room. It was short a bed for the three of them but far better than the motels and motor lodges she was used to.

"This my bed" Jersey Girl claimed and commandeered one of the two beds. Her alpha personality put her in charge of the trio. Plus, she would cut something.

"No funny business!" Country Girl laughed but only because she was down for the funny business. Mike often had them perform sex acts on each other if he used to much coke to participate.

"Yeah right!" the white girl laughed since they were practically a couple.

"Get a room!" Jersey Girl quipped then got down to business. She pulled her phone to go live and announce to their followers they were in the city.

Mike had arranged for a radio interview to make sure the beef was still simmering. The one sided feud was on its last leg so he paid the promoter to put them on the tour. He would get it back from the sales since he hardly paid the group anything. Their counterparts were worth millions but he gave them a weekly allowance like children.

"We need to get over to the station," Ki-ki reminded after their IG live where they danced around their room.

"Yeah," Jersey agreed and summoned an Uber. It was connected to the company credit card but would be deducted from their earnings. A few minutes later they arrived at Cleveland's hottest station. DJ Wiz Kid ushered them straight in.

"Alright Cleveland! I have a treat for you!" he hyped. "Jersey Girl, Country Girl and White girl Ki-ki. Otherwise known as, the Pretty Thugs!"

"Un-uh! We are the Real, Pretty Thugs! Don't confuse us with them bums!" Jersey corrected.

"For real boo-boo, they ain't us!" Ki-ki said, snapping her fingers with every word. Somewhere in time someone saw some black woman do that and it just went viral in real life. Especially amongst white women who want to be black and men who want to be women.

"There was some speculation about an incident in Atlanta? With C-money getting her face cut..." the DJ led.

"Ain't no spec, spec, uh that word!" Jersey Girl replied. She was as fine as a summer day is long but also dumb as a box of rocks. That's why she kept taking responsibility for a felony that even the victim hadn't reported. "I beat that ass and gave her something to remember me by. Err time she looks in the mirror it be like, 'hey!'."

※

"FUCK IT!" Callie said when she heard the dis about her face. The scar was barely noticeable but disrespect cuts deeper than any knife. She was saying fuck her career, money and freedom since she was going to kill Jersey girl.

"Now don't let her get to you! Don't feed into her bull shit!" Dominique urged. Twenty percent of nothing was a lot less than she was getting now, so Callie couldn't go to jail. She saw her hand go up to the faint scar once again. A habit she developed anytime their opps were mentioned. "Oh, doctor handsome said he'll see you as soon as we get back to Atlanta."

"Oooh, so you have been talking to him!" Penny sang. She too wanted to switch the subject from the wannabe thugs. There was too much money on the line to go out bad.

"Bruh, we finna be the last bitches standing!" Zenobia declared as Jovita stormed in.

"You hear this shit?" she barked and heard DJ Wiz Kid was coming through the radio.

"And we are supposed to be there later today," Dominique reminded.

"Man fuck that clown! He won't get props off of us!" she determined and that was that. Jovita didn't make many demands but she was the boss. So when she put her foot down the matter was settled. She warned everyone about fueling the beef that had already cost a few lives. Including the one she took by her own hand.

"Oh, he may get a few props off us," Callie mused and grinned wickedly. "He'll be at the show right?"

"Of course. He's the hottest DJ in the city," Dominique reminded as well. "A no show at the station could result in them pulling Pretty Thug songs from their platform. Which in turn cost us money."

"And still, fuck that clown!" Jovita repeated and set off a chorus.

"Fuck that clown! Un huh, fuck that clown! Say what, fuck that clown!" they rapped and danced and a song was formed.

"Wait, I know y'all aren't about to..." Jovita reeled when she realized where they were going with this. Alienating a major DJ in a major market could cost them millions. All eyes were on the boss to see if her foot went down. Instead she just walked away.

"IN CASE THESE HOES WANT SMOKE!" Jersey girl growled as she concealed a razor in her weave.

"I hope not," Country girl heard herself say. All eyes shot over to her as if she committed blasphemy. "What? Why do we gotta hate them? Just cuz Mike said so?"

"Cuz Mike said so!" Ki-ki proclaimed and confronted her like she wanted to fight. Mike fucked them all separately and collectively but she got hit the most.

"Un-uh! That's what we not gone do," Jersey demanded and stepped in between them before they went to blows. "Save that shit for the opps!"

"I ain't got no opps! I just wanna make some money!" Country girl whined. That was the heart of the matter as far as she was concerned. She followed the Pretty Thugs social media accounts collectively and individually and saw they were really getting rich. They actually generated a nice piece of change but all Mike gave them was the dick.

"We got a minute before this Uber come. Let's get high!" Ki-ki suggested. Mike did keep them supplied with pills, coke and weed to keep them high enough not to ask about their business. If they did they would see that he was charging them for their drugs as well. He invoiced every-thing except the air they breathed. They got good and high before the car service came to take them over to the arena.

"Ladies!" the promoter greeted them when the girls arrived on time. The fans were just filing in and the arena was filling up.

"Heeeey!" they sang and fell instep behind him as he led them to a staging area where the other opening acts were assembled.

"Um, where's our dressing room?" Jersey wanted to know.

"Yeah, no, opening acts don't get actual dressing rooms," he explained. Then pointed to the tables of food, "But help yourself to all the chicken you like."

"Ain't this a bitch!" Jersey fussed. "I'm calling Mike!"

"I'm finna, get me some chicken!" Country girl sang and rushed over with Ki-ki on her heels.

Jersey girl was armed and prepared for battle but they wouldn't get anywhere close to the stars of the show. Jovita had demanded they didn't cross paths and hired additional security if they did. They did their set, shot a few disses at their nemeses before being ushered completely out of the arena before the Pretty Thugs took the stage. DJ Wiz Kid was the MC of the show and had something to say about their no show.

"This next group needs no introduction, even if they did stand Cleveland up today! Maybe the Real Pretty Thugs were right..." he announced and whipped the audience up. He wasn't the only one with a mic though.

"Fuck that clown! Un-uh, fuck that clown..." the girls chanted a capella as they made their way out to the stage. Callie began to beatbox with her mouth while her girls tore the disrespectful DJ a new one.

Wiz Kid tried to shout over them but the show DJ cut his mic. He had no choice but to take the abuse while his hometown laughed at him. Callie provided the beat while her friends talked about his clothes, his voice and haircut. They saved the best for last since she had a speech to give.

"That's right Cleveland, fuck that clown!" Callie shouted and the massive audience thundered back. 'Fuck that clown!'

"Bet I don't play a second of y'all music ever again!" he vowed and stormed off to tens of thousands of people chanting, fuck that clown.

"And fuck whoever ain't us! Either you with us or against us!" Callie shouted and the crowd shouted back. 'We with you!'

"Naw, cuz some of y'all following us and them imitation hoes!" Zenobia barked knowingly because she checked. She literally spent hours verifying that some fans were playing both sides of the field. That wouldn't do at all and they let them know.

"So, whoever follows us y'all need to unfollow them!" P-money shouted.

"Or get blocked off our shit! On God y'all either thuggin with us, or slumming them!" Callie demanded.

"Look at this shit!" Dominique said and showed Jovita

her screen. They literally watched the imitators lose thousands of followers in real time. That was just the tip of the
iceberg. Once this video went viral they would lose a couple
hundred thousand followers.

"Oh, and I got a trick for that DJ!" Jovita snickered. She
sent out emails to all their sponsors demanding they pull
their ads from the station if he followed through with his
threat.

The word was out, the Pretty Thugs were not to be
fucked with.

CHAPTER 3

"Yo, that shit was crazy!" Callie declared the next morning when she emerged from her room. Only because room service had arrived. Not having to pay out of pocket made it free and she still didn't turn down free anything.

"Facts! Niggas want smoke, they get smoked!" Zenobia laughed and pulled the dome off the platter of meat. A pretty display of two kinds of sausages and bacon was neatly laid out. It smelled as good as it looked but not to her. "Ugh!"

"What?" Penny asked when her friend retched. "Girl you turning green!"

"I know the fuck not!" Callie growled when Zenobia rushed from the table and into her bathroom. The sounds of her throwing up carried through the otherwise quiet suite.

"What's wrong?" Dominique asked when she came out of her room.

"Z pregnant!" Callie snapped like she wanted to fight about it.

"She what!" Jovita shouted as she rushed out as well. She was busy negotiating deals worth millions for the group. This was the last thing they needed in their lives.

"Pregnant?" Penny answered and asked in the same breath since Zenobia was returning.

"Bitch ain't no one pregnant! The smell of all that meat just made me sick to my stomach!" she shot back.

"See, that's why Ion mess with that swine!" Dominique said and hoped it was settled.

"Sensitivity to smells and morning sickness?" Jovita asked since she knew the clinical symptoms. Penny nodded along since she knew them first hand. Zenobia did too except for one important fact.

"But I ain't been fucking! Y'all may have forgotten, but my man got killed," she retorted sharply.

"And you've been with Pretty Boy every night, every city!" Callie dared.

"You clocking my coochie now? I ain't fuck that nigga! Shit, that nigga was snorting so much powder he can't even get his dick hard!" Zenobia replied hotly.

"Good thing you ain't got a dick!" Callie said.

"Fuck that supposed to mean?" Zenobia wanted to know and stood. Callie was with whatever she was with and stood as well.

"Both of you calm down! Sit down and eat!" Jovita shouted them both down. The stress of the road was wearing on everyone. She was the boss so she made a boss decision. "We have a few days between the next shows. I'm going to have the jet fly us to Atlanta!"

"Yay!!" they all cheered since there is no place like home.

"I'M ABOUT to order food. Are you eating?" Callie asked Zenobia when they got back to their apartment. The offer of food was her way of apologizing.

"Wings?" Zenobia asked which meant she accepted it.

"Mix lemon pepper and volcano, all flats," she laughed, knowing what her friend wanted. Best friend at that so she offered a full fledged apology. "My bad ma."

"We good. We just needed a break," Z said and dapped her up. She had been pregnant before but no way was this that. She still pulled a spare pregnancy test left over from Young Vaughn. She peed on it before she came out so it would be negative by the time she returned. A high pitched howl interrupted their talk.

"The fuck was that?" Dominique asked as she came out of her room. They got their answer a few moments later when Penny staggered from her room on wobbly legs.

"Whew! I needed that!" she laughed after a bout with her Rose. Her friends got a good laugh but Dominique had a date with some doctor dick.

"That reminds me!" Callie snapped her fingers and rushed into her room to call Ervin.

"Lemme see what this thang 'talmbout..." Zenobia sighed as she checked the pregnancy strip. She twisted her lips at the plus sign and wondered what it meant. She dug the box from the trash and checked the instructions. "How the fuck..."

"Them wings on the way..." Callie was saying but Zenobia was in a trance. She waved her hand in front of her face and called, "Hello?"

"You good girl?" Penny asked. It was she who saw the test strip in her hand. "Nuh-uh!"

"Yeah, but I ain't been fucking? You think it could be him? Vaughn's?" she moaned. Callie and Penny shared a glance to see who would take that question. Vaughn had been dead for months but she was so adamant about being celibate. They could see the wheels turning in her head so they remained mute and let her work it out. The emotions on her face morphed from confusion to wonderment, to enlightenment and finally anger.

"What girl?" Penny asked when Zenobia began to cry. It was a slow build but soon she was beyond words and had to be consoled. Her friends swooped her into a group hug and held until she got it out.

"That's what the fuck he meant," Zenobia recalled Cousin Vinny's words came back to her.

"Who! What!" her friends wanted to know.

"Vinny, Pretty Boy cousin! He tried me up after he got killed. Then, said some shit about, I let him hit before!" she relayed.

"So, you didn't fuck Pretty Boy but gave his cousin some?" Callie strained to understand.

"Hell naw! But I passed out over there one time," she admitted. "Then, the next day I was sore like I had sex. But I didn't have sex. Lavonda told me Pretty Boy had left for a while and Vinny came into the room. That nigga raped me!"

"And his ass is going to jail!" Penny growled.

"Naw, his ass getting beat the fuck up!" Callie corrected.

"Girl I ain't trying to have my business all over the damn inna-net!" she shot back.

"I feel you girl. He is not getting away with this shit! On God he's gonna get his!" Callie vowed. This wasn't the best time to have the other she and Penny decided to have with her. She decided to have it anyway. "You gotta slow down ma!"

"Word! I get partying, but you ain't a rock star!" Penny added. Zenobia wanted to shoot back but didn't have any ammo.

"Y'all right. I'ma chill," Zenobia sighed. She had spiraled out of control and it was time to reel it in. Penny and Callie nodded since that was easier than they thought it would be. Only because it's never that easy.

"YOU LOOK CUTE!" Penny gushed when Callie presented herself for inspection. Tonight wasn't a photo op so she wasn't wearing any of the brands that paid her. Tonight she was after something more substantial.

"Just cute?" she whined and pouted. "I was going for slutty."

"You need to hit my closet for slutty," Penny snickered.

"This will have to do," she sighed and smoothed her tube dress. The skin tight garment wasn't exactly wholesome either since it showed every curve. Plus the fact that she didn't have on a lick of drawers. "I just hope ole boy eats pussy."

"They all eat pussy chica," Penny reminded. At least that had always been her experience. Even the loudest ones who protested about how they don't eat pussy and don't kiss in the mouth. Then, as soon as they get her alone they eat the pussy like a condemned man's last meal.

"True. I meant to say I hope he can eat pussy properly," Callie sighed. It was time to head out so she texted her friends the address and headed out.

The GPS directed her to a quaint block a block away from Grant Park. New money had given the old homes new life and outrageous property values. She pulled in front of a million dollar bungalow and checked herself in the mirror once again.

"Pssssh!" she huffed at the waste of time since she was just as cute as when she last checked. She reached for her door handle but Ervin was already there to pull it open.

"Hey th...." he was trying to say when he held her door open. He accidentally looked between her legs as she stepped out and got mesmerized by her magnificent vagina. It was freshly shaved and pleasantly plump.

"I know right," she laughed and stood. They shared a peck on the lips before he took her by the hand and led her inside the house.

"Shall I give you the tour?" he offered as she looked around the immaculate living room. The difference between old money and new was evident in the details. The classic craftsman features were blurred by modern furnishings.

"After," she replied and grabbed his crotch so he wouldn't ask any stupid questions like, 'after what?'.

"After work," Ervin agreed and scooped her up over his shoulder like a caveman. She giggled girlishly when he dumped her on the bed.

"Un-uh, slow..." she directed when he began to undress. He laughed and made a show out of coming out of his clothes. Meanwhile she just squeezed out of the tube dress the same way she squeezed into it. She clapped when he finally revealed the dick. She had quite a few pictures of it from their conversations while she was on the road but they didn't do it justice.

The dick would have to wait though since he slipped face first between her big brown thighs. A loud hiss filled the room when the tip of his tongue first touched her love button. A few flicks had her writhing and squirming like a freshly dug up worm.

Ervin upped the ante by lifting her legs by the ankles and twirling his tongue. She tried to shimmy away but got trapped by the headboard. There was nowhere else to run so she just gripped the sheets and held on. Not for long though since an intense orgasm was creeping up on her.

"Dang boy!" she screeched and let loose the juice as she bust a nut in his mouth.

Ervin sat up and replaced his tongue with his fingers. He slid one in and out of her slippery box while tearing open a condom with his teeth. He rolled it down his dick right before Callie grabbed it and guided him inside of her. She used to fuss when Voodoo lifted her legs by her knees but tonight she pulled them back herself.

"Mmhm," her lover agreed and delivered the dick. Their tongues twirled in each other's mouth and stifled their mutual moans.

Ervin thought about baseball, fishing, NASCAR and business as he gave her the business. Anything to keep his mind off the vice tight, juice box he was deep inside of. None of it worked though and the end was near. He usually had pretty good stamina but she got the best of him.

"Fuck!" Callie grunted and bust another nut on the next down stroke. It was the last down stroke since he went stiff and filled up the rubber. They both moaned and gasped for air from the climax. As soon Callie could speak she announced, "Round one!"

It was going to be a long night.

CHAPTER 4

"Man..." Zenobia groaned when she saw the familiar building.

"I'm here shawty," Penny declared as she pulled into the parking lot.

"I'll hit you when I'm ready," she said before Penny could open her door. She was dressed down so she wouldn't be noticed but P-money stood out wherever she went. The last thing she wanted or needed in her life was the insult to injury of this going global.

"Before you go in, so I can be here when you come out," she insisted and didn't budge until she agreed.

"OK girl," Zenobia said and double checked her disguise. She tugged at her wig and fiddled with her large shades before getting out.

A different guard manned the door and confirmed the alias name Zenobia was using. He asked for ID and confirmed the dead president on the hundred dollar bill. The press of a button buzzed the lock and granted entry into the abortion clinic. The fake name was waiting at the desk where she was given a number. Once again the number preoccupied her thoughts as she waited her turn.

All heads still rose and turned each time the door opened. Then lowered when they didn't find the salvation they hoped for. Zenobia looked up and down with each opening and closing as people came and went. She had been there for an hour when a familiar face walked in. Zenobia froze as the young woman walked over and traded her name for a number. She looked like she was in a daze as she came and took the empty seat right next to Zenobia.

Zenobia wondered if the girl was trying her but she didn't even register her or anyone around her. She just stared down at the number in her hand to wait her turn. Finally the heat on the side of her face from the stare made her look.

"Z-money?" Country girl asked, almost afraid.

"Shsssh," she shushed since she was undercover. The abortion clinic specialized in abortions but she still asked, "What are you doing here?"

"My CEO don't like to use protection and don't like to pull out," she fussed. This was her second time here aborting Mike's children. Jersey girl had to abort one as well but Ki-ki usually swallowed so she was safe.

"Dang!" Zenobia reeled when she processed that. Then processed the fact that she admitted it to her since they were supposed to be beefing. "I guess we'll have to call a truce until we finish our procedures."

"Chile I ain't got no beef with none of y'all! Mike put us all together and promised to make us famous. Ion even like them hoes!" she admitted and laughed. It was contagious and Zenobia got caught up in it as well. Come to find out laughing out loud in an abortion clinic is more egregious than talking in the library. All eyes landed on them which made them laugh even more.

"Tiffany," Country girl offered along with her hand. Zenobia extended hers to shake it, then quickly snatched it back.

"Hole up, y'all jumped my girl tho. And cut her face!" she remembered.

"Mike made us, but your girl whooped all our asses. Jersey was the one who cut her. I wasn't with that," she confessed. Zenobia pondered for a second, then took her hand. They found out they had more in common than they thought. Including a love of pills, coke and weed. They exchanged numbers before Zenobia was called in first to remove the wanted child.

"WELL HELLO LADIES!" Jovita cheered when she met the group for dinner. Everyone looked rested and happy. "I see the idea of coming home did the trick!"

"Yeah, cuz I got some doctor dick," Dominique agreed.

"I got my boots knocked real, real good!" Callie added happily.

"I fucked myself but it's still nice to be home for a sec," Penny said. She had run through a four pack of double A batteries but sleeping in her own bed seemed to recharge her internal battery.

"I seen my granny!" Zenobia sang. She left out the part about copping some pills while she was over there. She also ran into the same pack of hood rats who almost jumped her and Penny. Now they treated her like a celebrity and took pictures with them. Zenobia smoked some weed with them and exchanged numbers.

"Good. I'm glad because we leave in the morning," she informed.

"Make mine to go please," Callie requested and pulled her phone.

"Me too. Matter fact," Dominique cosigned and stood. We walked off and went to get some more doctor dick before leaving the city.

"We with you!" Penny declared on behalf of herself and Zenobia.

"Speak for yourself," Zenobia laughed and stood. She headed out and back over to the hood to hang out with chicks who never wanted to hang out with her before.

"I'M HOME!" Mike called out as he entered the condo he put the girls up in. He could have had them share a one bedroom but didn't. He still billed them rent and board along with anything else he could add to separate them from their money. The whole thing was his idea so he figured they would take what he gave them. The group actually generated millions from riding on the Pretty Thugs hype.

"Shit," Country girl groaned when she heard him from her bedroom. She flipped over and pretended to be asleep so she wouldn't have to deal with him.

"Hey daddy!" Ki-ki said and went straight for his zipper.

"Where is Tiffany?" he asked and brushed her hand away.

"In her room. She stay in her room!" Jersey girl snitched as if keeping to herself was a crime. She had definitely been doing that since the blow up and even more since the abortion clinic.

"Yo," Mike demanded as he entered the room without knocking. It wouldn't hurt to knock but he needed to prove he didn't have to. He did have to repeat her name and shake her to wake her.

"Huh? Oh, hey. I was sleep," she fawned and yawned to make it seem true.

"You handled that?" he growled since she seemed a little reluctant when he told her to have another abortion. It would certainly be easier to wear a rubber or pull out. Especially since he wasn't the one with his feet in stirrups having a person vacuumed out of his uterus either.

"Yeah," she whined. He put his hand between her legs and felt for a pad to confirm, just like she knew he would. He Still pulled his dick just like she knew he would as well. "I just had a dang abortion!"

"That's cool. I ain't want no pussy," he shrugged and pulled her down by the neck.

"Can I please get some money? For my mama?" she asked on her way down.

"I'm tryna get my dick sucked and you talking about your mama. Shit, I should go over there. Since she needs some money," Mike sniped with his nasty ass. He didn't even notice the tears from her saliva as she complied with the forced felatio. It's been said you can lead a horse to water, but can't make them drink. Mike couldn't eitherand Tiffany spit a fresh batch of baby batter back out her mouth.

"Tuh!" she spat and grimaced. Her head shook when she finally tasted that this wasn't worth it.

"Let all that good protein go to waste!" he laughed and stood to put his dick away. "Come out here so I can talk to y'all."

"You straight daddy?" Ki-ki asked when he emerged since she was horny herself. Mike made them save it for him while he tried to singlehandedly fuck the city of Atlanta.

"I am, but y'all got a flight to catch," he said and handed out their tickets to the next stop on the tour. "Sales are slowing down too. Y'all need to step up y'all game. Run up on stage on them bitches! People love that shit!"

"Word, we on it!" Jersey cosigned.

"Them hoes scared, but we gone find a way!" Ki-ki agreed since she agreed to anything Mike suggested. Country girl had nothing to say since she was just biding her time. The promise of money kept her around but she planned to bounce as soon as she got it.

THE NEXT STOP on the tour right up 85 to South Carolina. Technically they could have driven but still used the promoter's jet. The imitators flew coach with screaming babies and angry Karen's fussing over mask mandates. They ended up at the same arena but the promoter made sure to keep them separate. Still there was some ruckus outside their dressing room.

"What the hell is going on out there!" Callie wanted to know when the commotion outside their dressing room got louder.

"Dang groupies prolly," Zenobia guessed. Whatever it was would have to wait since she slipped into the bathroom. She quickly whipped out a cellophane package and smiled at the glistening powder inside. Her manicured nails made the perfect spoon to snort cocaine. This wasn't Raisin Bran but she did take two scoops and inhale up each nostril. "Whew Chile!"

"Man!" Penny grunted and snatched the door open to find out what was going on. She saw the burly security struggling to keep a girl back. She was amused at the young chick giving the man fits until she got a good look at the face. "Wait!"

"She said she's with you guys?" the man huffed, out of breath from the struggle.

"She is! Let her through!" Penny demanded and threw her arms wide to receive the blast from the past. "Hey girl!"

"What was all that?" Zenobia asked and wiggled her nose with her finger like Bewitched, except she wasn't Samantha, she was back on the powder.

"This lil girl..." Penny announced and stepped aside so their guest could be seen.

"Lacrecia!" Callie and Zenobia shouted and rushed over to hug her neck.

"What the hell are you doing here?" Callie wondered.

"Girl, my daddy calls himself sending me to my granny. Caught me riding some dick in the driveway!" she laughed. It hadn't been quite a year since they saw her but they all noticed she had aged at least a decade. This wasn't the sweet, little country girl they dubbed 'lil girl'.

"In the driveway tho?" Zenobia laughed since she wasn't going to judge.

"Hell yeah," she began and paused to light a cigarette before continuing. "This one nigga I been fucking stay with his baby mama. He drove me home from the club so I fucked him. My daddy call himself waiting up on a bitch and got an eye full! I was just busting a nut when he pulled the door open!"

She laughed at her own predicament and blew a plume of smoke toward the ceiling. The blank looks on Penny and Callie's faces didn't even register before she went on. Lil girl was gone, this was a grown woman.

"My daddy is a damn hypocrite tho! Act like my grand-daddy ain't eating all that coochie round town. Done ate all my lil friends!" Lacrecia laughed. "My granny mad cuz I ain't enroll back in school so I was staying in a hotel."

That was just part of the problems she was having with her grandmother. Not wanting to enroll in school was just part of her problems. Her budding drug problem was also a problem. Oh, and dick. Once she got her first piece of dick she got addicted.

"You're staying with us now!" Zenobia declared. "We need an assistant anyway."

"Y'all want me to slap them fake thugs for y'all?" Lacrecia offered since everyone followed the beef.

"Naw, they don't get no props. They lil light finna fizzle out," Zenobia declined. It was but she also felt bad for Tiffany. The young woman was trapped and didn't know how to get free.

A tap on the door announced show time so the Pretty Thugs went and gave the people what they came to see.

CHAPTER 5

"So, what are we supposed to do with her?" Penny asked Callie as they headed back to the hotel. Lacrecia and Zenobia guzzled champagne in the limo.

"We? Nothing. I on got no kids," Callie shrugged and went back to texting her boyfriend. It was official like that, with a label.

"Let's fire this up!" Lacrecia cheered and removed a blunt from her purse. It was just one of a few drugs in her bag.

"Hole up. They don't smoke," Zenobia declined and rolled her eyes as if smoking was better than not smoking. The world is fucked up like that now. Bad is good and good is scorned.

"Where is she staying?" Dominique asked. The question inferred the answer that she wasn't staying with them.

"I'ma get her a room," Zenobia shot back, then turned to her friend. "I got you Lil girl!"

The limo arrived at the hotel and Zenobia marched defiantly over to the reception desk. She didn't have a credit card or even ID but she was a Pretty Thug. The clerk had no problem with booking her a luxury room a few floors down from the penthouse.

"Five hundred dang dollars!" Lacrecia reeled at the rate. She had been shacking up with different dudes in thirty dollar a night joints.

"Hell yeah! I'm up, so you up!" Zenobia declared and headed for the elevators. "Shit I make ten racks err time I smile for the cameras!"

"Dang!" the girl repeated in awe at the numbers.

A second thought made her make a second call. She gave the receiver the room number and hung up. The key card opened a whole new world to the naive country girl. Zenobia knew exactly how Lacrecia felt as she ran around the swank room.

"Wish we had some powder!" Lacrecia proclaimed once they settled on the sofa and lit a blunt.

"I ain't no Jeanie or nothing but..." Zenobia laughed as she granted that wish by producing some cocaine. She dumped it on the table and began to make lines when a knock on the door lifted their heads. "Get the 'doe lil girl!"

"Oh! Yeah!" she laughed and rushed over to pull it open. The smile on her face flipped when she saw the opp on the other side of the threshold. "Fuck she doing here!"

"Cuz I invited her! Now let her in!" she fussed. Lacrecia snarled at Country Girl as she came into the room.

"Call her off," Tiffany laughed and took a seat.

"She's cool. Loyal as fuck. Took a bullet for us," Zenobia recalled, even though her friends seemed to have forgotten. The fact of the matter was that everyone was changing. Money and fame has that effect on everyone. Some good, some bad. Some major, some subtle. But everyone is sure to change.

"That's what's up," Tiffany nodded in response to her and the blunt being passed. She accepted it and took a deep pull.

"So, what's up with this?" Lacrecia asked, pointing between the public rivals who seemed to be quite cool in private.

"Cuz, I ain't with all that drama!" Tiffany said between tokes. "I met Mike 'ndem in the club. Next thing I know, we in a dang rap group!"

"Yeah we got more in common than people know," Zenobia said since they shared a secret.

"Mmhm," Tiffany hummed since she still harbored a secret of her own. She watched as the two girls eagerly snorted the lines of powder off the table.

"Have some? We got plenty!" Zenobia offered when she saw her looking.

"Huh? Naw, I'ma stick to the weed," she decided. She did like to party hard but knew she needed to fall back for a few months. "Oh! Y'all gotta watch y'all back! Mike 'sposed to be tryna pay somebody to let us on stage in one of these cities. He says we need to fight so our sales can go back up!"

"Say less," Zenobia replied and began to plot herself. If that's what he wanted she was going to help it along but it wasn't going to play out like he thought.

"NEXT STOP, TUCSON ARIZONA!" Dominique cheered happily as they boarded the private jet. She was always excited to visit places she had never been. Especially since they were getting paid six figures to come.

"Grrrr," Zenobia growled at the mention of the city.

"Oh yeah! That's where ole boy is from huh?" Penny recalled.

"Was from," Callie corrected since Pretty Boy was dead. His cousin Vinny still lived there though. Plus he was living his best life from his cousin's death.

"He needs to go with him," Zenobia added.

"I'm sure I don't need to hear this conversation," Jovita said and pushed her ear buds in deeper. The label was on fire since the Pretty Thugs blew up. Now they had several acts in the studio recording. She would check their progress over them plotting someone's demise.

"Wish we could call Alizae..." Callie suggested. She tossed it out the same way a fly fisherman tossed his line, to see what bites. No one did since Alizae was too volatile to handle.

"Can I help?" Lacrecia offered. Smiles lit the cabin of the jet as a plot came together. Callie thought she might balk at the plan after what she had been through but that person didn't exist anymore. This new chick was down for the get down.

A limo awaited the group in a private hangar when the private jet arrived. It whisked them away to a resort villa where each Thug had their own bungalow. There was a couple of days before the show which meant radio visits and photo shoots. Plus plenty of time for some well deserved get back.

"You ladies get some rest. We're on the morning show

bright and early," Jovita announced as they made their way to their units.

"Okay!" they all sang even though none of them meant it.

Ervin would be landing in an hour so Callie had plans to ride him forward, backwards and from the side. Penny would be going live to address her legions of fans. She now had more followers on her personal page than the group's page. Even she didn't see how that was going to her head. Meanwhile Zenobia was spinning a web to catch a spider.

"HELLO?" Cousin Vinny asked skeptically when he took an unknown caller on his private line. Everyone who had this number was entered into his contacts so this call almost got ignored.

"Oh, now you don't know a bitch!" Zenobia barked into the line. "Never mind, bye!"

"I thought you was finna..." Lacrecia was asking in confusion but Zenobia held up the ringing phone to prove her point.

"Hello!" she snapped, rolled her neck and fluttered her eyes as if the caller could see her.

"Who dis?" Cousin Vinny needed to know. He had fucked every one in his contacts so some new pussy intrigued him immensely.

"Nigga, now I know you heard the Pretty Thugs was in yo city and you acting brand the fuck new!" she fussed.

"Z-money!" he cheered when he finally caught the voice. It wasn't exactly new pussy but having her consent and actually participating would definitely be new.

"In the muhfuckin flesh! And I'm trying to hang out tonight," she offered.

"Swing through!" he cheered and began canceling his other plans.

"Shoot me the address and we'll fall through if a few," she agreed and hung up before he could ask who was the we she spoke of. He shot the address via text and the web was set.

"You sure this gonna work? What about if he don't like me? How we finna know if it works?" Lacrecia worried. She was down for anything to help her friend.

"Don't worry, it's gonna work," she assured and passed her a pill to pop. Plus the drink to wash it down. Lacrecia shrugged and took her word for it. She swallowed the pill and waited for it to work. By the time they arrived at Vinny's gated estate she was definitely feeling it.

"Hey!" Vinny cheered and threw his arms open to hug his favorite victim. He had stolen a lot of pussy thus far but she was his only celebrity. That was destined to change since he had a slew of young artists vying for his attention to blow them up like his dead cousin.

"Nice place!" Zenobia cheered after the embrace. In an instant she made the decision to buy her own place when they returned to the city. "This is my little cousin Lacrecia."

"Hey," Lacrecia greeted. She managed a smile even though she was woozy from the pill and the drink.

"Well, hello little cousin," Vinny greeted as they entered. He also noticed that little cousin had thick thighs and a lotta ass. He also saw her wobble slightly on the heels she wore.

"Party favors!" Zenobia sang when she saw the buffet of drugs laid out on the coffee table. She leaned in and snorted a line of each nostril before lighting a blunt. Lacrecia made a move for the cocaine but didn't make it. "Un-uh lil girl! You have some weed and get you a sip but you are too young for that!"

"Let me get some more ice," he said and left just long enough for Zenobia to set the trap.

"OK," Lacrecia pouted and took the blunt and drink. A few rounds and she was leaning to the side.

"Little cuz done tapped out," Vinny said while looking at her legs. He was hoping they would separate enough to let him see between them.

"She ain't but sixteen! Tryna hang with the..." Zenobia was saying until her phone buzzed on her hip. Her eyes went wide when she read the text that came through. "Shit!"

"What's up?" Cousin Vinny asked, hoping whatever it was wasn't going to prevent him from getting some pussy.

"Shit I forgot we had a shoot! I ain't got time to take her drunk ass home and damn sure can't take her with me, like that..." she pitched.

"Just leave her! You can come back and get her when you handle your business," he offered and hit it right out of the park like she expected.

"You sure? I'ma be at least an hour..." Zenobia pouted.

"Yeah, I got you," he assured and caught an instant erection. Zenobia acted like she didn't see the lump in his pants as he left her friend to the wolf. Lacrecia agreed to take one for the team and this was the one.

"An hour, I'll call as soon as I'm on my way!" she said over her shoulder as she rushed back out to the rental.

"OK! I got you! I'll take good care of her!" Vinny called and waved until she was out of sight. He turned back inside and closed the door behind him. Then looked at the sleeping girl from head to toe. "Where do I begin..."

The question was purely rhetorical since he knew exactly where he wanted to begin. That required lifting her hips to help ease her panties off. The cartoon characters on the underwear only added to the narrative of her being sixteen and that made his hard dick throb that much harder.

He began to dip between her legs but stopped to undress her completely. That didn't take much doing since he only had to lift the dress over her head and unhook her bra. Lacrecia's nineteen years wasn't that far off from sixteen so he didn't know the difference. Her vagina sure didn't taste any different that he could tell. She may have been sound asleep from the interaction of the opiate and alcohol but her vagina still responded to being licked and sucked. The combination of seduction and saliva soon had her slippery wet.

"You wanna return the favor?" he asked and rubbed his erection against her lips. They parted with her soft snores and he pushed himself inside. After a minute of dead head he climbed between her thick legs and worked his way inside. He pulled her legs onto his shoulders and picked up the pace. The first nut came quickly but he stayed hard and went for another.

By the time Zenobia returned with the police he had filled her young box completely full of his DNA. He had dressed her again like nothing happened but it all happened while the camera Zenobia set up recorded it. Cousin Vinny was going to prison for a long, long time.

Lacrecia popped a morning after pill after the rape kit that would seal the rapist fate, then never spoke of the ordeal again.

CHAPTER 6

The tour snaked its way up, down and around the United states. The album had just crossed the four million sales mark and spawned two number one hits. More endorsement deals flooded in for the whole group but Penny still received double what the group did, while Callie received twice as many as Zenobia did. Only because she didn't promote and engage at the rate of her friends. She was more interested in partying in every city they stopped in.

The fake Pretty Thugs were barely hanging on. The promoter moved them up to the first act as their demand began to fizzle. Mike was livid that they couldn't get close enough to pick a fight and get some free publicity. Not only were their sales plummeting but they couldn't get along. Tiffany spent more nights in the spare rooms Zenobia kept for Lacrecia than with her own group. Mainly because her secret was now impossible to keep.

"Girl, what the fuck!" Lacrecia proclaimed when she saw

Tiffany's bare belly. She had managed to hide the baby bump for a whole trimester but there was no hiding it now.

"A baby is the fuck," she laughed. A knock on the door interrupted the conversation for long enough to let Zenobia in to take them to lunch.

"Girl, what the fuck! Your ass knocked up again?" Zenobia reeled. It wasn't long ago that they bonded in an abortion clinic.

"Not again, Still," she corrected. The correction still needed explanation so she expounded. "Man, I ain't finna keep going through all that! Mike likes to nut in hoes then send us to abort the babies. I did it once, I'm not doing it again!"

"So you must have left before I came back out?" Zenobia guessed. She wasn't in the waiting room when she finished her procedure so she assumed she was in one of the stalls getting vacuumed out as well.

"I sat there for a few minutes and said fuck this shit," she revealed.

"So, what the daddy finna say?" Lacrecia wanted to know. She didn't know all the players but followed along as best as she could.

"We finna find out cuz I'ma tell him today. I'm done with this music shit. I'm going home to my mama," Tiffany determined.

"Good for you!" Zenobia declared. "Now let's go eat!"

"And then shop?" Lacrecia asked hopefully. She too had gotten bit by the shopping bug since they hit malls and boutiques in every city. Zenobia preferred to spend money on clothes instead of wearing the brands that paid her to be worn. Then again she stayed pretty high every day.

"And shop lil girl!" she laughed. Tiffany wasn't seeing much cash from her career so Zenobia bought her clothes too. Some days she managed to spend as much as she made.

"THE FUCK YOU BEEN?" Jersey Girl asked when Country Girl made it to the room. She didn't spend any nights with the crew and only showed up for shows.

"Never mind that! What the fuck is that!" White girl Ki-ki reeled and pointed at her belly. Tiffany rocked a sheer shirt that was open at the bottom to show off her baby bump like Rhiana. She didn't have time to wait for the obvious answer since she was a slave. "I'm telling Mike!"

"Good idea," she chuckled since it would save her from having to do it. Ki-ki called on video so she could show and tell.

"What! You found a way to get on stage with them bitches? That must be the only reason you calling since I told you not to call me until you found a way to get on stage with them bitches!" he barked as she turned the screen to show the baby bump. "The fuck is that? Bitch is that why you can't find a way on stage? Too busy fucking niggas on the road!"

"Only nigga I fucked is you," Tiffany said calmly. There was a moment of silence while they all processed what that meant. She had been a hoe since puberty but this was the first time she actually felt like one.

"So, what you do with the grand I gave you for an abortion!" he wanted to know because he was petty like that.

"Told you my mama needed some money. Ain't like we seeing much money from all this," she explained. That required another moment of silence to process since the other girls felt the pinch of being broke. Ki-ki and Jersey both did better fucking ballers they met in the club. Which was how they met Mike and got caught up in this whirlwind. He sold them all on the dream but the reality was becoming a nightmare.

"I dripped you bitches in the latest fashion and jewelry! Don't be ungrateful!" Mike snapped.

"But you billing us for everything we get! You got us beefing with chicks who are making millions!" Tiffany moaned. The reality of the disparity hit a nerve with one, but not the other.

"I had to pawn my chains to send my little sister some money," Ki-ki revealed.

"Y'all really some bum hoes!" Jersey spat. "Mike put us on and y'all hating on the man!"

"Naw, I don't hate him," Tiffany said softly. "If anything I feel bad for him. Don't worry about the baby. I'm good. And after tonight, I'm done with this."

"Where she going? Get back here bitch! Bitch!" Mike screamed.

"She's gone," Ki-ki moaned and secretly wished she could have gone with her. She actually knew she was hanging out with Zenobia since she saw her in the background of a post. Plus, she had a lot of new clothes and Mike certainly wasn't giving them money.

"Ungrateful ass bitch!" Mike snarled. His twisted mind quickly spat out an answer to his problems. "Tell y'all what. Y'all bitches want money? I got twenty bands for y'all to bum rush the stage tonight!"

"Consider that shit done!" Jersey quickly agreed. Where

there's a will there's generally a way but add twenty racks on top and that shit will get done.

"Fuck yeah!" Ki-ki agreed too since she needed some bread. All he had been giving her was meat and now she was late for her period too.

"Oh, and I got another twenty to beat the baby out that dirty bitch," he dared.

"That shit is done too!" Jersey agreed and Mike was gone.

"Ion know about that girl," Ki-ki moaned. "I'm down to fight them hoes, but a baby? Naw, I aint about that shit!"

"A dead baby. I'm getting that bread!" Jersey girl replied.

"HE SAID WHAT!" Zenobia laughed at Mike's reaction to the paternity news.

"Girl! The nigga was more worried about the money for the abortion!" Tiffany reeled and shook her head. "See, I was just gonna raise my baby by myself. Now I'm finna hit his ass up for all kinds of child support!"

"I cain't stand niggas!" Lacrecia snapped.

"Lil girl, what you know about niggas!" Zenobia laughed. She and Lacrecia debated back and forth while Tiffany took a call that left her pale.

"What's wrong!" Lacrecia asked when she saw her face.

"You look like you just seen a ghost!" Zenobia whined.

"I did. The ghost of my baby!" she sobbed and held on to her stomach. It took a few minutes before she was able to compose herself enough to pass along what Ki-ki just revealed to her.

"Good!" Zenobia snarled wickedly. "I gotta bounce. I'll see y'all before the show!"

"Um, OK..." Lacrecia said as she rushed from the room. She always booked the extra room in the same hotel so she wouldn't have to go far.

"Look what the cat done drug in," Callie said when Zenobia bust into the penthouse.

"Yeah, we can do that later. Right now we have bigger issues..." she said and filled them in.

"Let's just go to their hotel and bomb on these bitches now!" someone suggested. Everyone was surprised to see it came from Jovita.

"Well, if boss lady say bomb, let's bomb!" Dominique shrugged. They would have gone over there and done just that if Callie hadn't hit the brakes.

"Nah, I got a better idea," she said and ran her finger along her scar. "They want attention. Wanna rush the stage. We gonna let 'em!"

"I FOUND A WAY," Tiffany whispered in a conspiratorial tone once she was backstage with her group. Those were the first words spoken through the thick tension hanging in the air.

"For what?" Jersey whispered back since she was whispering.

"To get on stage. There is a trick ass security guard who asked about you," she continued. White girl Ki-ki looked on in wonderment.

She was actually surprised the girl didn't make a run for

it after she told her about the bounty Mike put on her baby. Jersey wasn't even thinking about rushing the stage anymore. She wanted the easy money and planned to kick Tiffany down a flight of stairs. Then jump on her belly with both feet if need be.

"Word?" she asked wide eyed as another twenty bands presented itself. She listened intently as she filled her in. She then filled Ki-ki into the real plan when Jersey called Mike to fill him in.

"Check..." Ki-ki laughed and gave Tiffany a pound. She smiled and gently touched her baby bump. There had once been hostility between the two but it vanished in an instant the baby moved. "It moved!"

"Yeah, it does that," Tiffany laughed. She transformed into Country Girl when the DJ announced their set.

"Let's do this shit!" Jersey cheered and led the way out to the stage. They ran through their mediocre stage show to a half filled arena. The people were still arriving since there was still plenty of time until the stars took the stage. People were here for Z-money, C-money and P-money.

The growing crowd did applaud when they saw Country Girls' baby bump. Jersey played along but still planned to kick it out of her for twenty thousand dollars. She still had another surprise planned and Mike had given her the green light since the tour was coming to a close anyway.

"Play that shit!" Jersey announced and the beat to the dis song began to boom through the arena.

"We not supposed to do that one?" White girl Ki-ki asked since she wasn't on the call with Mike.

"I'll do it my damn self!" she laughed since he planned to give her a solo deal anyway. Jersey girl stepped to the front of the stage and launched a nasty personal attack on the Pretty Thugs over the beat while her group mates slinked off stage.

"NOW DON'T REACT! I'll handle it!" Jovita pleaded as she entered the dressing room while the slanderous song played through the arena.

"Handle what? React to what?" the Thugs asked as their whole lives were being mocked. Jersey girl proved herself a solo artist when she rapped the whole song by herself. The crowd ate it up because people love bullshit and drama.

"That song? Ain't nobody thinking about them bum broads!" Callie said dismissively. Jovita looked at Dominique who looked as shocked as her since she had no clue what was coming either.

Jersey repeated the line about cutting Callie's face over and over after the music was cut. All eyes shifted to Callie who didn't flinch. She usually subconsciously touched her face but this time just kept on texting back and forth with her man. Zenobia and Lacrecia headed to the table full of food to load up. She made sure to eat well before starting to get high for the night. Cocaine is a hell of a drug and zaps the appetite.

Meanwhile, security met the real Pretty Thugs side stage after their set to escort them away from the venue as usual. The promoter was determined to keep them away from the headliners so they couldn't fight.

"I got them Truck," a new guard announced as he came over. Truck squinted at his name tag before acquiescing.

"OK, Nate," he agreed since he wanted to get back to the

groupies. A few of them would do strange things in strange places just to get close to the artist. "Straight out!"

"Straight out!" Nate agreed adamantly, then did the exact opposite. "This way..."

"Hells yeah," Ki-ki cheered as they dipped into another secure area behind the stage. They still had a couple hours to go until the Pretty Thugs took the stage. Nate has ideas on how to fill the time.

"You ready to take care of me?" he asked Jersey directly.

"They ain't paid you? Y'all ain't paid him?" Jersey asked between her friends since this was their thing.

"Girl I told you dude tryna get with you!" Country girl sang and wiggled her eyebrows. Jersey blinked a few times to process and sighed. She had too much money at stake to turn back now.

"Come on with it!" she said and squatted before him. "Your dick better not stink!"

"It don't?" Nate guessed and whipped it out. Country girl and Ki-ki backed up enough to give them some semi-privacy. Still close enough to catch the scene clearly on their phones. They caught the blow job in stunning HD. Even the gulping climax was caught clearly.

"Shit, come on with it..." Jersey decided and lifted her short skirt, then bent over a chair. She wasn't used to going so long without dick but Mike didn't touch her during their last stop over in Atlanta. He had some chicks in the bed when she spoke to him earlier so she decided to get some dick on the road.

"Bet!" Nate cheered and slid right up in her. Country girl happily recorded more incriminating videos but the best was yet to come.

"Coming to the stage..." the radio personality announced when it was time for the stars of the show to take the stage.

"Shit!" Nate grunted when his play time came to an end. He pulled out and put his dick away wet while Jersey girl prepared for battle by lacing her Timberland boots tight.

"Ki-ki, you better take Z-money and let Country Girl fight the white girl since she is pregnant," Jersey directed.

"OK!" they both responded quickly. Jersey girl may have been a hater but she was still a fan so she rapped along with every song. Even did the Money Dance when it came on. When the Pretty Thugs neared the end of their set they snuck behind the stage to bum rush.

"Y'all ready?" Jersey asked rhetorically, then led the charge.

"Sike!" Ki-ki snickered as she and Country girl stayed put.

"Oh, look who's here!" Z-money cheered.

"Right on time too!" P-money added since they were waiting on her.

"What the fuck is happening here? Someone tell me what's going on!" Jovita demanded.

"I have no idea?" Dominique asked as well. Luckily for both, Callie was about to explain.

"This bum hoe here has been begging for my attention! Now she got it! Bitch cut my face in Atlanta when it was three on one. Now we about to shoot a one" Callie said and passed off the mic.

"Oh you want these hands bitch!" Jersey girl laughed, but should have been swinging because Callie was done talking.

'Pap. Pap, pap-pap' the straight jabs sounded off each

time Callie popped her. All the slap boxing sessions with Voodoo came back as she picked the girl apart.

Jersey was a brawler, throwing wild haymakers that Callie easily dipped and ducked. Each one cost her another pop in the mouth. She realized her opponent had superior hands so she dipped low and rushed in to take Callie down. Turns out that wasn't the best idea either since Callie shot her a knee that stood her right back up.

Now it was Callie's turn to swoop low. She scooped Jersey into the air and above her head. The crowd went wild, screaming to finish her. Callie slammed her down with all she had which proved to be enough since the girl was out cold.

'Finish her!' the ravenous crowd screamed like a Roman arena. Callie lifted her own Timberland above the woman's mouth to knock out her teeth. It was only the look of shock and horror on her friends' faces that saved the girl tens of thousands on dental work.

"She's already finished," Callie said over her shoulder and walked off the stage. The arena was eerily quiet for a full minute until a slow clap started somewhere in the sea of people. P-money and C-money took a bow and rushed to catch up with Callie.

"I don't know what happened? I gave instructions! I'll get to the bottom of this!" the promoter pleaded to Jovita but she lifted her head since she already said what she said.

"Let's go back to the hotel and pack. We're going back to Atlanta!" Jovita said, and the show was over.

CHAPTER 7

Back to Atlanta meant getting back to work. Jovita had quite a few offers and deals on the table but gave the girls a couple weeks to be girls before she would summon them to the office. They all had plans to fill that time off. For Zenobia that meant finding some space where she could do her. She took Lacrecia along since she would be staying with her.

"This bitch is bad!" Lacrecia declared. The excitement made her dig her menthols from her purse.

"Can you not do that?" the realtor asked nicely. Then ignored the eye roll since the girl closed the purse. She initially wondered if this young client could afford these half a million dollar condos but she knew Gucci when she saw it. Zenobia may have gotten paid to wear her sponsor's clothing but she still spent lavishly on clothes, shoes, purses and drugs. Not just for herself but she sponsored Lacrecia and her habits as well.

"This bitch is bad tho!" Zenobia agreed. The four

bedroom unit was near the top of the high rise building and overlooked her city. "I'll take it."

"Great!" the woman cheered for the high commission she just scored. "We can go to the office and start the loan process and..."

"Naw, we can go to the bank and cut a check!" Z shot back. She and Lacrecia cackled and high fived.

"I know that's right!" Lacrecia cheered as if she had a dime to help with the purchase price. In truth she didn't have a dime to her name, except what she received from her friend. Luckily she had a generous friend with deep pockets.

"It's settled then," the realtor said and led the way from the unit. "I'll let the manager know you're on the way back to the office. I have another appointment."

"Bet that," she agreed and led her friend from the unit. She had the purchase price and headed to the bank to pull a certified check for the full price.

The realtor stepped out on the balcony and retrieved her vape pen from her purse. It was loaded with a cannabis cartridge so she took a few pulls as she looked over the city. She would have taken a few more but her next client called from the parking lot.

"I'll be right down!" the woman sang and scurried from the unit. She popped a mint in her mouth for the ride back down.

"Miss Turner?" the client asked when she approached.

"Yes, but call me Alice!" she replied warmly. For the potential commission on this unit this woman could call her anything she wanted.

"OK Alice, I'm Penny!" Penny cheered and extended her hand. Once they made each other's acquaintance they headed up to the top floor. The penthouse units went for seven hundred and fifty thousand but Penny wasn't paying cash. Her accountant set spending limits to limit the chances of going broke.

"Ok Penny, let's go view your new home!" the saleslady said like a saleslady says. She led the way back inside and up to the nearly million dollar unit with the million dollar view. That's why she had the tri-fold doors already opened wide.

"Oh my!" Penny reeled as she saw the view of the city. She rushed out to take it all in. It must have been enough since she spun and announced, "I'll take it!"

"Don't you want to see the bedrooms! The ensuite is like a spa!" she vowed.

"Um, sure. But I'll take it," Penny insisted and followed her around the unit. It only had three bedrooms but they all had the same spectacular view of the city. Penny repeated herself again in each room. "I'll take it!"

"NO NEW CRIB FOR YOU?" Dominique asked since everyone else was buying property. She enjoyed her time with the girls but had copped a half million dollar townhouse for herself.

"I wish the fuck I would when this place is paid up for the rest of the year!" Callie shot back. Not only was she cheap, it just went against her sensibilities to leave the apartment when the rent was paid up.

"Girrrrrlll!" the woman laughed and shook her head. It made too much sense to dispute. "Plus, you don't hardly even be here..."

"Only cuz I'ma cowgirl. I be across town riding dick. Backwards!" she cackled wickedly. In fact she had only stopped in to reload her 'spin-a-nite' bag.

"This is getting kinda serious huh?" Dominique inquired.

"I stayed over while I was on my period," Callie nodded since that's pretty serious. Especially when she wasn't going down on him yet. If a dude still wants to spend time and nights with a woman without any sex it's because he enjoys more than just her sex. He enjoys her company.

"Damn!" Dominique reeled at the revelation. She and the doctor were getting pretty close but she took a week off when aunt flo came calling.

"I know right," she laughed along with her. The mood was casual enough but they had business to attend.

"So, I got a few inquiries about a solo deal..." she revealed.

"What about the second album?" Callie wanted to know since her loyalty was to her friends.

"That's first but, it's good money," Dominique laid out and waited for the question.

"How much?" she asked like Dominique hoped she would.

"Three million! It's a 360 deal but once they recoup, it's seventy, thirty. Your way," she explained.

"I thought you said no 360?" Callie asked in confusion.

"I did, but at least we see what you can bring on the open market. Jovita should match it," she replied. "If the second album does at least as good as the first I'm looking for five mil for your solo project."

"Yeah, plus I would have to talk to my girls first," she sighed. The thought of leaving them took the joy away from the few million dollar prize.

"Yeah..." Dominique agreed, but left out the offers P-money was receiving. Zenobia would fetch a pretty good solo deal too but Callie and Penny were the top draw.

"I'm surprised ole girl ain't cracked the whip yet?" Callie wondered. Jovita gave them a week off but it has almost been two.

"She has. Group meeting tomorrow," she said as she stood.

"Where are you going!" Callie snapped as if she wasn't going somewhere herself.

"Um, auntie is a cowgirl too!" Dominique laughed. "Yee ha!"

"SLOW DOWN LIL GIRL! We ain't even made it to the club yet!" Zenobia chided as Lacrecia guzzled her glass of straight liquor.

"Un-uh! Turn up!" the teen cheered and leaned in to snort one of the lines off the table. Zenobia just shook her head but only because she couldn't see the girl was trying to be like her.

"The limo here," the star announced when she received the text alerting her of the car's arrival. She had been doing some dumb shit since she had been home but at least she was smart enough to let someone else drive her to and from it.

"Let's ride!" Lacrecia said as she stood. The lines of cocaine on the glass table beckoned once more so she bent over and inhaled another. One of her titties fell out the top of the skimpy dress when she stood. "Now, I'm ready!"

"Yeah, no. I'ma need you to put yo titty up tho," she

laughed and popped the breast on the way out of the unit. Zenobia stopped at the door and admired the condo before locking it up. Fucking up or not, this was one thing she did right.

"Yo shit tight girl!" Lacrecia confirmed and they set off for a night on the town.

"Miss Money," the driver announced with a nod as he held the door open for his client for the evening. He was her carriage for the night, to take her wherever she wanted to go.

"Miss Money!" Lacrecia snickered as she slid in first.

"Thank you, Donnel," Zenobia read off his name tag. Then dropped the name of the hottest club in the city. "The Red Light!"

"Yes ma'am," he said with another nod as she slid in the back seat. He had a clear shot of her bare vagina but didn't take it. This was Atlanta after all and not every man in this city likes vaginas. Some dudes have a penchant for penis. Donnel was some dudes.

The car company had a no smoking rule but rich people do what they want. That's why Donnel just opened the windows and sunroof when the smell of weed wafted up front. The club was downtown near their condo so he wouldn't have to endure it for long.

"Turn that up!" Lacrecia demanded when a Pretty Thug song came on the radio. Being from this city meant one of their songs was playing on one of the stations at any given time. P-money's appeal even granted them access to some of the less melinated stations as well.

"Whooooo!" Zenobia howled as she stood out of the open sunroof when the car turned on the block the club was located.

"Ooh! It's Z-money!" a woman in the long line squealed and set off a frenzy.

"Hey y'all!" Zenobia cheered and waved at the adoring fans. Not long ago she would have hopped out and partied on the sidewalk with them. Now all they got were waves and kisses as they pulled to the front of the venue. Donnel passed on another crotch shot as he held the door open for the ladies to exit.

"Just text whenever you stand up at your table to leave. I'll be right here when you step out that door!" he assured her. Just because he didn't like pussy didn't mean he wasn't professional.

"Dang! OK!" Zenobia reeled. She was still getting used to the star treatment.

"Hello Z-money. Would you like to join your friend?" the manager greeted as he took the handoff of the VIP guest from the driver.

"Who my friend?" she shot back

"P-money already up in there!" Lacrecia answered for him since Penny had just gone live.

"Um..." she hummed until she saw the pack of rats from her old hood in the line. "Naw, give us our own table. And let my friends in!"

"Right away!" the man agreed. He nodded his bouncer in to collect her friend while furiously tapping directions into his phone to ensure a table was cleared by the time they arrived.

"Hey! Thank you! Love you too! Awe, thank you girl!" Z-money worked her way through the club. The manager and another bouncer cleared the way like offensive linemen for a running back. She spotted her band mate holding court at a table and made her way over. There was no beef, they just required their own shine. Sometimes egos grow too big to share the same spotlight. The old timers call it getting too big for your britches. "P-money!"

"Hey Z! Y'all make room for my girl!" Penny directed to the people surrounding her. She didn't call any of them by their name since she didn't know them.

Just more movers and shakers looking to attach themselves and their companies to the P-money train. Jovita booked her to hang out with the business folks who had been blowing her lines up. Including one with a manufacturer in China ready to print up some P-money panties since a crotch shot up her skirt went viral. Only because she ironed her name right on the sweet spot. The two dollar heat transfer was about to net her millions.

"Sup P-money!" Zenobia cheered, hugged, kissed and smiled for the cameras. It looked great but was genuine too since they did love each other. Not to mention not having seen much of each other since returning to the city.

"Sit! Hang out!" Penny offered.

"Girl, I got a 'huned dang people with me!" she declined. It was a slight exaggeration since only about ten chicks were with her. It would definitely grow before the night was over.

"I see!" Penny laughed. "I'll see you at the meeting tomorrow girl!"

"OK! Yeah! Mmhm!" she replied as if she hadn't completely forgotten about the meeting. They hugged once more before departing.

"What y'all mean I gotta get up! I'm Bobby Brown!" the singer protested as he was carried away from the table. Proof you're only as good as your last hit and his was before Z-money was even born.

"Don't be cruel!" Zenobia snickered as he was taken away.

"Ooh that ain't right!" Lacrecia laughed and shook her head.

"That's why I'ma always be a star!" Z-money declared as the waitress arrived. "Brang us, ten bottles of moèt! Two bottles of Henney and two bottles of Alizae!"

"We don't..." the waitress was saying until the manager shook his head. They didn't serve Alizae but he tapped into his phone and an assistant took off to the liquor store to get some. "Coming right up!"

"Ooh girl, ain't that John 'Flash' Peters!" Lacrecia shouted and pointed at the star point guard from the Hawks. He was a light skinned pretty boy with a reputation with the ladies. Every week he was linked to another actress or singer.

"Mmhm and him look gud!" Zenobia grunted just as the man turned in her direction. They locked eyes for a moment before he turned away and headed for his own table.

"Un-uh! No he didn't!" one of the hangers on announced at the perceived snub.

"Girl, this is Atlanta!" Zenobia reminded and told them about the driver. They were cackling real good when Flash appeared at the table.

"Excuse me ladies..." he interrupted and looked them all over before settling on the star. "My name is Flash. I'm a big fan!"

"Want her to sign an autograph on yo dick!" Lacrecia slurred since all those drugs and all that alcohol had caught up with her young ass.

"Hey Flash! I seen you play! I'm a fan too!" she replied warmly.

"I see you're having fun, but why don't you call me sometime?" he offered along with his card.

"As long as this ain't to the hoe phone," Zenobia laughed as she accepted the number. She may have laughed but was still serious.

"Let me see?" he said and checked the number on the card. "No, that's my direct line. Hit me up."

"I'ma hit you up a'ight! Grrrrr!" she growled at his back as he walked away.

Penny popped through on her way out just after midnight but the party was just getting started for Z-money and her crew. She went live and did shots with fans from around the world. The sun was rising rapidly by the time they stepped out of the club the next morning. Donnel whipped up to the entrance when he spotted the entourage emerge from the club.

"Take me home! Then take them wherever they wanna go," Z-money directed as she led the pack of rats into the limo.

"Don't forget you got a meeting!" Lacrecia reminded.

"I ain't. Finna get a lil sleep first tho..."

CHAPTER 8

"Hello there!" Jovita sang jovially when Callie arrived at the office. Her eyes glanced up at the wall clock to confirm what she already knew. There were a few minutes to spare since the young woman was always early.

"Good afternoon ma'am," Callie replied all business like. Obviously that tickled because she let out a little giggle. Jovita smiled since it was refreshing to see her happiness. The hard young woman she met nearly a year ago was beginning to soften. Just a little, around the edges.

"Ladies..." Dominique greeted as she breezed into the conference room from her office down the hall.

"You're in a good mood!" Jovita noticed and smiled. Because positivity and happiness are infectious. That's why it's so important to keep miserable, negative mother fuckers as far away from you as humanly fucking possible. Callie knew why she was in such a good mood though.

"She's a cowgirl," Callie informed. "Me too. We ride bulls."

"OK, and I'm going to schedule counseling sessions for the both of you because..." Jovita joked as Penny entered like a diva. Her Prada heels clicked loudly on the floors while Prada shades covered most of her face.

"Good morning ladies!" she greeted with her nose in the air. The room went quiet for a moment to see if she was serious. Her shooting star could drag her ego right along with her. It wasn't until she lifted the shades to show her eyes were crossed that they realized this was still the same old Penny.

"Hey girl! Where's Z?" Callie asked when she didn't come in behind her.

"Ion know?" she shrugged and took her seat.

"Wasn't y'all both at the Red Light last night?" Dominique asked even though she knew they were. Penny was entertaining suitors while Zenobia went live while she partied like a rock star.

"And that's where I left her," Penny shrugged again. It was more pronounced this time to clarify that it wasn't her problem.

"Hmp?" Jovita hummed and wondered if she didn't need to have separate meetings with the group. The fissures were evident and could only widen.

"Well, the meeting has begun," Dominique declared and proceeded. "The first album was a smashing success. That means we need to have the follow up like yesterday!"

"Indeed! We need to strike while the iron is hot! Even though I never quite understood the analogy?" Jovita added.

"Like a blacksmith. I saw a documentary..." Callie informed since she knew a little about a lot. Everyone knew this about her so they let her explain the blacksmithing analogy.

"Unfortunately the tour ended abruptly but the demand has actually increased. My suggestion is to go back out and finish what we started," Dominique suggested.

"The P-hive got a hundred thousand votes to come to Iowa, Utah, Dakota..." Penny informed.

"The fuck is a, P-hive?" Callie wanted to know.

"Her fan base. Five million and counting," Jovita replied. The question and answer brought her to her next point. "The demand for solo albums is growing. Offers are pouring in."

"I already know! Method man said he wanna do a song with me!" Callie cheered.

"Yeah and Death Trap reached out to me to do a song with Penny for his album. I told him he can be on her album," Jovita huffed.

"He's the biggest crossover rap/rock star in the country!" Penny proclaimed and pumped her fist. The mulatto man appealed to both races and took full advantage of it in his music.

"He's the biggest alright," Dominique laughed since the eccentric star just went viral for showing his dick recently.

"Must have got the dick from his daddy," Callie guessed since his father was black.

"I have no idea where the notion of...never mind," Jovita began, then stopped. She and Penny shared a glance since they once shared the same dick and Ethan held his own in the dick department.

"Anyway," Penny cut in since she was done talking about dick. "So, what y'all talking about on the next album? And a solo album?"

"Same split. You ladies are getting rich as is. Why change anything?" Jovita replied.

"What about the solo deals? Y'all ain't tryna beat all offers?" Callie asked and looked to Dominique. It was a good time for her to reveal the offers she had received.

"Well, Def Jam is offering three million to sign Callie," Dominique revealed.

"We'll match it!" Jovita quickly shot back, then turned to Penny to offer the same. "And three million for your solo album."

"I want five. I deserve it. I have five million followers," P-money informed while Penny sat back. The true statement bounced around the quiet room for a few minutes before anyone could speak.

"She ain't no bigger than me! I want what she gets," Callie said directly to Dominique since she was her manager.

"Let's take a step back and focus on the second album. The sophomore jinx is a bitch!" Jovita chimed in. This was no doubt going to be messy and she didn't want to deal with it publicly. Back office deals would have to be made in confidence and kept quiet.There were smaller offers on the table for a Z-money solo deal but she wasn't here to hear them.

"I got my shit ready!" Callie challenged across the table to Penny.

"Same here! Let's get it!" P-money accepted on behalf of Penny. It was nice to have an alter ego ready to speak for her at all times.

"What about Z? Where is she?" Dominique asked again just as an assistant rushed in with the answer.

"Z-money is on TMZ!" the woman shouted and aimed the remote at the large TV.

'Rapper Z-money of the Pretty Thugs was caught on hotel security camera snorting an unknown powder up both nostrils...'

The video was from the hotel elevator. Once it was discovered it was shared privately until someone sold it and it went public.

"Oh no!" Callie moaned as she watched the video repeat itself.

"Welp. That's gonna cost her," Dominique said and shook her head. The Pretty Thugs didn't have the most wholesome image but this wasn't a good look.

"Maybe," Jovita said, twisting her lips. The sad part about it was that Zenobia's stock would go up because of this. Because people are some bullshit and love the bullshit.

"FUCK! THE FUCK!" Zenobia grunted when she stirred awake the next afternoon. Once she sat up she realized her door bell was ringing constantly. Now she just wanted to know who the fuck was ringing her bell like that, this early in the damn morning. Until a glance at the clock revealed morning had come and went hours ago. "Fuck!"

Lecrecia was in a coma of her own until the doorbell woke her up. She was just too spoiled and selfish to get up and answer it.

"Ain't for me no way," she huffed and flipped over as Zenobia stomped by, down the hallway.

"OK, OK!" Zenobia fussed and pulled the door open to find Callie. "Dang!"

"Dang my ass!" Callie fumed as she barged in on top of her. She looked around to see if she could see what was more important than the millions on the table back at the office. Her lips twisted and head shook at the liquor bottles, weed clips on the coffee table. She couldn't see the cocaine residue left behind from the lines snorted off it. "You bugging yo!"

"Bugging how? I overslept!" she shot back and shrugged dismissively. Meanwhile Callie tried to figure out the fancy remote so she could turn on the fancy TV. Now it was Zenobia's turn to shake her head and lean in to help out. The remote was voice activated so she said, "TV on!"

"TMZ," Callie told the TV and it flipped to the station.

"Hey Callie," Lacrecia croaked when she came out in search of water to quench her cottonmouth.

"Mmhm," Callie shot back. She had no talk for either of them until she saw what she wanted to show them.

"Girrrllll!" Lacrecia moaned when she scrolled through her phone.

"What!" Zenobia said and came to look over her shoulder. They both watched her image sniffing coke in the elevator.

"Here it is!" Callie announced when Zenobia popped on the huge TV screen.

"Dang!" Zenobia reeled and paused to see how she felt about it. Her shoulders shrugged before the words came out of her mouth. "Fuck it."

"So, fuck the group huh? For our show money?" Callie snapped. "You may not care about a solo deal but you are still part of a group!"

"You right. My bad. That was right after I saw Pretty Boy get killed," she guessed and nodded at the good excuse. "I was messed up."

"I guess," Callie agreed. She certainly should have been messed up behind the murder. Even though she sure seemed calm when they reached her at the crime scene. "Cool, I'll remind Dominique so she can spin it. You need to go see Jovita about your bread!"

"You right. My bad mama. I'm finna get it together. No more coke or pills," Zenobia sighed and embraced her friend.

"Um, OK? Good!" Callie said and joined the hug while Lacrecia looked on in confusion.

"Let me call Jovita now," she said as they broke off the embrace.

"Cool, cuz I got a rodeo to tend to," Callie said over her shoulder as she headed back out of the condo.

"Roll up my nigga!" Zenobia ordered once they were alone again. She fished out a bag of coke from her bag and dumped it on the table.

"But, I thought you just said..."

"I said what she wanted to hear!" Z laughed and inhaled two lines of coke. They were the first lines for the day but would not be the last. "And let me call Flash and see what this nigga 'talmbout..."

"HEY JOVITA, I was just finna call you!" Zenobia lied when she took the call she forgot to make. She had every intention of calling after Callie left but started getting high instead. Then she kicked it with Flash who was now on his way to pick her up for their first date.

"Yeah well you didn't. Now, you have two choices," she said firmly. "You can either meet me at the office now..."

"Or?" Zenobia asked when she didn't give the second option. She had already made up her mind to take door number two since she had a date. Her vagina was freshly shaved and legs oiled and glistening.

"That's it. Option two is that's it. Find new management," she replied plainly. There was a terse silence while the stubborn girl contemplated. Jovita opened her mouth to make the decision for her but Zenobia beat her to it.

"I'm on the way. On the way out the door!" she relented on her way out the door. She hung up and left instructions over her shoulder. "Flash finna be here in a few minutes. Have him wait. I won't be more than an hour!"

"I got you girl!" the youngster cheered. She was always eager to carry out any instruction or task.

Lacrecia looked at the lines of coke left on the table and figured she needed to get them up before company came. They went right up her nose before she wiped the table clean from the residue. She dumped the full ashtrays and put the glasses in the dishwasher right before the bell rang.

"Shoot!" she fussed since she didn't get to change from her around the house clothes to something more appropriate for company. The bell rang again so she went to let the man in. She snatched the door open and cheered, "Hey Flash!"

"Hey," he greeted in reply then grimaced at the plump breast holding the halter top up above her bare belly button. His eyes fell between her legs and landed on the fat camel toe on display in the tiny shorts.

"Come on in. Have a seat while I go change," she said and turned to run off and do just that. Only problem was those brown ass cheeks hanging out the bottom of the shorts.

"Hold up!" he called after Zenobia told him to stay put until she returned. "Don't leave me by myself."

"Um, OK," she relented since she was still a little country girl at heart. She joined him on the sofa but gave him plenty of space.

"I don't bite," he assured and patted the empty space next to him. "Might lick or suck, but not bite!"

"OK," she said and slid over next to him.

Flash immediately reached between her legs and rubbed that fat camel toe. Lacrecia just looked down at his hand like she didn't know what to do. He did though and slipped his fingers under her shorts. Her vagina knew what to do too and soaked his fingers.

"Dang!" Lacrecia moaned when the stimulation made her whole body jump.

"Damn!" he agreed when he slid a finger inside of her. He looked at his hundred thousand dollar watch to see how many minutes was left in that hour Zenobia said she would be. Math was never his strong suit so he just whipped out a rock hard erection.

"Dang!" she repeated and touched his dick. She pulled her hand away and giggled like a girl.

"Come on..." he urged and pulled her down to the throbbing erection. She turned her head and had dick pressed against her cheek.

"Ion suck no dick," she moaned and pouted. The once good girl had just started fucking recently, so sucking a dick was still nasty to her.

"Damn!" Flash groaned because his dick was too hard to go back in his pants. His finger was still gripped by that tight little box though. "Fuck it!"

Lacrecia wasn't sure what to do or say when he laid her on her back. So she said nothing when he lifted the shirt enough to suck the hard little titties. Nothing when he began to pull the tiny little shorts off. That required a hip lift so she complied. He lined his dick up with her young box and plunged inside. That got something out of her.

"Ssss! Owe!" she hissed and moaned as he filled her with dick. He slid his tongue into her mouth to hush the hiss.

He was too excited and she was too hot, too wet and too tight for this to last too long. Clock or no clock that good, young pussy rushed him along. He may have gotten ten strokes in before the electricity began shooting through his body. Up his legs, through his brain, then straight out of his dick.

"Fuck!" Flash moaned as he pulsated and skeeted in that good, young pussy. He pushed as deep as he could and filled her up before slumping over.

"Um..." Lacrecia said, thinking he was going to sleep.

"Yeah," he said and withdrew from her vagina. His dick was all wet and shiny from their combined juices. "Where's the bathroom?"

"First door, on the right," she pointed. He wobbled down the hall with his still erect dick leading the way. He could go another round but there wasn't time. Plus, he still had a date tonight.

CHAPTER 9

"He Zenobia greeted solemnly when she entered the office. This was actually sincere since she really looked up to Jovita.

"Hey yourself. Have a seat," Jovita said and waved at the chair in front of her desk. She had the form withdrawing from her management filled out and signed. All it took was Zenobia's signature to be a done deal.

"I know you seen that video. That was..."

"Right after the murder. I know. Callie told me," she revealed. Zenobia smiled internally at her friend's intervention. Then felt bad for lying to her. "What I'm worried about is you! Forget business, what do you need?"

"Someone to talk to," Zenobia pouted. Her lip quivered as she fought back the tears. "I just be going through shit and keep going like nothing happened. Seen my daddy kill my mama. Blew her brains out,"

"Oh my God!" Jovita moaned. She knew the story not the

details and there was no fighting her tears back. She rushed around the desk and scooped her into an embrace.

"I just be taking it! Like it's OK!" Zenobia whined as Jovita squeezed her tightly. So tightly she couldn't see the girl roll her eyes. Yeah, she had been through a lot which made her just not give a fuck. One day all that real grief would really hit home like a ton of bricks. Hopefully she won't have burned all of her bridges when it does.

"Well..." Jovita began once again after Zenobia regained her composure. She retook her seat behind the desk and switched back into business mode. "First things first. We need to get you guys back in the studio for your follow-up album."

"Come on with it! I'm ready! I got songs, on songs, on songs!" she vowed and danced in her chair as proof.

"Good," she sighed since that was settled. The others were on board so now she could book some studio time. "All three of you have had plenty of interest in solo deals."

"I'm with that too! I..." Zenobia cheered but didn't reach the end of the cheer.

"A few of them pulled their offers after the video surfaced," she stated plainly. Zenobia mentally sighed and got ready to play victim again but again the woman beat her to the punch. "Don't worry about it. It'll all be forgotten once the second album is done and you guys do your tour. And, we'll still match any offer to keep you here, at home."

"I'ma tighten up! Watch, I'm finna do better!" Zenobia vowed. This time she was sincere for a reason. "And, I met a guy. We have our first date tonight!"

"Good! Have fun, have sex, have desert, whatever!" Jovita

directed. "Have a good night's sleep because you're in the studio tomorrow!"

"SHIT, see how long she's gonna be..." Flash suggested as he and Lacrecia sat on the sofa pretending to watch the TV like they didn't just fuck. He hoped he had enough time to fuck her again before his real date.

"OK," Lacrecia agreed simply because she was still green enough to do whatever she was told. She reached for her phone but it buzzed before she could get to it. She looked at Flash when she took the call with a, "Where you at?"

"Pulling up now," Zenobia replied and parked next to Flash's Bentley coupe. On a whim she decided she wanted one as well. Money was to be spent so she planned to spend some more.

"She on her way up?" she reported and waited for instructions.

"Shit, I prolly could hit that tight lil box one more 'gin!" he laughed at himself. With that preliminary nut out the way he was ready to give her the business.

"Yeah, cuz you was Quick Draw McGraw in this thang!" she teased and laughed. He laughed along with her but only because he planned to punish her young ass next time he fucked her. And they both knew there would be a next time.

"Hey y'all!" Zenobia sang as she entered her condo to the sound of laughter. "What's so funny?"

"He a trip!" Lacrecia cracked up some more so she wouldn't have to talk. She had changed into a pair of jeans and shirt but her panties had a glob of his kids in them.

"She took care of you?" Z asked as Flash stood to take her on their first date.

"Very good care!" he smiled. "You ready?"

"I'm ready!" she sang and led the way out of the unit. They headed down to his Bentley and over to one of his favorite restaurants.

Dinner was filled with conversation and laughter as they got to know each other. They had a lot more in common than they realized including incarcerated fathers. His was a serial bank robber, to her convicted killer. Shared taste in music, movies and opiates.

"What was that?" Zenobia inquired when he attempted to discreetly pop a pill. It would have gotten by the average person but she was a pill popper herself.

"Oxy. I take them for pain management," he replied along with his excuse. She nodded with the familiar excuse she used quite often herself.

"Oh, I thought it was something to help keep your dick hard," she said with perfect timing. She waited for him to sip his champagne to see if he would choke. He did, and laughed.

"Trust me, this guy stay long and hard for a long time!" he vowed as if he didn't just bust a forty five second nut an hour ago. Only because with that one out the way the next one would be a long time coming like a Sam Cooke song.

"Check please!" Zenobia called and waved for their waitress. "I'm tryna see what that thang 'talmbout!"

"No, I got it!" he insisted when she thrusted her card towards the waitress.

"Naw, cuz if I pay for dinner you gotta put out!" she said and made the waitress laugh.

"Well, I'll pay the tip," he offered and pulled a roll of hundreds from his pocket. He made sure a card with the number to his hoe phone was with it when he handed it over.

"I should suck your dick on the way over," she thought out loud as they rode.

"You should!" he shouted and leaned back to get it out.

"Except, Ion suck dick like that," she laughed and teased. Not that she wouldn't, it just wouldn't be tonight.

"You got jokes!" he laughed since she was rare. She had good looks, a good sense of humor, a fine frame, and her own money. The perfect chick to sport on his arm. "I like that!"

"I like you," she admitted. The car went quiet to process until he reached his reply.

"I like you too. A lot," he confirmed. That didn't mean he was going to stop fucking her friend though.

"SHIT!" Zenobia reeled when she awoke in Flash's bed. She popped her head up and looked at the clock. She was so used to waking up well in the afternoon she was relieved to see it was only ten. "Whew!"

"What time you gotta be there?" Flash asked. Not that he necessarily cared, he just hoped he had enough time to fuck her again. To his delight she was as right and tight as Lacrecia was. He caught some flack about his short relationships but most of those famous chicks had big vaginas from fucking their way up the ladder.

"Right after you make me cum one more time," she said, reaching for his dick. He reached for another rubber as they began to kiss. His dick responded to their making out and her hugs. They kept right on kissing while he rolled the condom down his dick. He rolled on top of her to put it in but she pressed pause. He literally devoured her vagina last night so she wanted a little more head. "You not finna kiss it, again?"

"It's gonna taste like latex and spermicide 9000!" he laughed since they used multiple rubbers last night. It made sense so she un-paused and gave him some pussy.

That morning wood served them both well. Flash made her come in a flash and pounded out a nut for himself before they hit the shower. Once they were clean and dry they headed out so Zenobia wouldn't be late for the session.

"Just drop me off at the studio. I'll have Lacrecia bring me some clothes," she decided when she realized there wasn't time to go home. She would not be late again.

"Who?" Flash asked since he forgot the girl's name already. He remembered that hot little juice box, just not her name.

"Lacrecia! My lil sis. You sat with her last night," she reminded.

"Oh yeah! That's right, Lacrecia," he laughed and repeated the name to lock it in. "Lacrecia, Lacrecia."

"Shit!" she fussed when a nag reminded her that she needed a pill. "I need a perc or something."

"Say less," Flash assured and popped the glove box that doubled as a pharmacy.

"OK, you my boyfriend now," Zenobia laughed and plucked a few pills. Some for later to go with the one she swallowed down with saliva. The small talk continued until they reached the studio. They leaned in and made out like boyfriend and girlfriend in the front seat until a knock on the window startled them both.

"Get a room!" Penny fussed and knocked some more. It was clear she wasn't leaving without Zenobia so their make out session was over.

"Lunch?" Flash asked as she reached for the door handle.

"Shit, we just gonna be warming up by lunch," she sighed. Recording a song can take minutes or hours depending on different factors.

"Dinner then," he insisted and got another peck before she closed the door. Flash wore a brilliant smile as he pulled away from the studio. Mainly because he liked this Z-money, but also because, "I'm about to go fuck the daylights out of Lacrecia!"

"OK, what's this?" Penny demanded as they headed inside.

"A lil sum, sum," she replied nonchalantly but the broad smile on her face said it was a lot of sum, sum. Both heads turned as the crazy person blaring their car horn as they pulled in. The car screeched to a halt and the crazy person jumped out.

"What y'all cheesing about!" Callie demanded as she rushed over.

"Z got a boyfriend!" Penny informed her.

"Oh yeah! Speedy!" she recalled.

"Uh, Flash," Zenobia corrected.

"I hope he don't fuck in a flash," Penny grimaced like that would be tragic.

"Nope. Knocked the boots like a champ! I started to pour champagne over his head!" Zenobia cackled. They entered the studio laughing and smiling and all the recent animosity had dissipated.

"The thugs are back!" Malik cheered when the Thugs

entered the room. He was pleasantly surprised they were right on time.

"We're back!" Callie cheered. They all migrated to their usual spots around the room as he began playing the different beats from different producers to pick from. That proved to be a problem.

"Oooh! Dassit!" Callie jumped to her feet and cheered when a beat caught her attention. "That's some up top flow right there!"

"Yeah, and I'm ain't!" Zenobia laughed and shook her head. "I want some trap music!"

"I'm looking for something more mainstream? Salsa infused, rock, something. What I don't want is to make the same album we just made!" Penny informed.

"You mean, like the four times platinum album that spawned four top ten hits! Including a number one?" Malik asked even though that was the answer.

"Whatever yo. Just save that one for my solo joint," Callie dismissed. The tone was set and each girl picked out more beats for their solo projects than the sophomore album.

CHAPTER 10

'Gawk! Gawk! Argh! Gawk!' Ki-ki squawked each time Mike slammed into her larynx. She knew this wasn't about pleasure, he was trying to pain her. Doing it in front of Jersey girl was meant to humiliate her. He had her head propped on the pillow so he could fuck her face.

She decided she would take it as penance for abandoning Jersey and letting Callie beat her down in front of the whole world. The Pretty Thugs had quite a few fights caught on video but this one had the most traction. Dominique capitalized on it by uploading an official version with a blow by blow commentary from Callie herself. It was generating tens of thousands of ad money from the video sites.

Mike left her stranded and made her find her own way back. Tiffany got enough money from Zenobia to fly them both back. She went home to her mother to have her baby but Ki-ki had no mother or home to go home to. So she ended up knocking on Mike's door, asking for Mike's forgiveness. Which was how she got put in this position to be punished by Mike's dick. It had been a couple of weeks and he still hadn't spoken to her except to fuck her throat.

"Mmhm!" Mike growled as he pressed his full weight on the dick down her throat. It pushed tears from her eyes when it cut off her air. Mike was on the verge of choking her with the dick before he pulled out. "Flip over!"

"Un-uh!" Ki-ki declined which made everything to follow rape.

"Un-uh like you left your girl on stage to get jumped!" he snapped and flipped her over on her stomach forcefully.

"Pain her ass daddy!" Jersey cheered even though she wanted some dick herself.

Mike spit on her box even though it was good and juicy already from him fondling it. She just gripped the sheets and gritted her teeth when he plunged inside of her. Once again there would be no tenderness. Mike slammed in and out of her with everything he had. Only problem was, that's how she liked it.

"Shit!" Ki-ki grunted and now gave her consent in the form of an arch in her back. It allowed him to reach a little deeper in her gushy insides. Jersey girl frowned when her moans of pleasure picked up. She was really hot when Ki-ki shivered and shook when she came all over the dick digging her out.

"Fuck!" Mike announced and snatched out. His chicks knew he only pulled out for one reason so Ki-ki flipped back over and scrambled to get him back in her mouth. Plus it was less work than the abortions he kept sending them to have. Ki-ki gulped louder than necessary to show her submission.

"Mmmm, mmhm," she hummed as she sucked him dry.

Mike humped her face a few times before roughly snatching himself out of her mouth.

"So you think that makes up for your treachery?" He asked and cocked his head like a dare.

"Hell naw! Bitch stood there and let me get jumped!" Jersey girl spat hotly. Part of that heat was because of the good piping she just watched when she was horny herself.

"Ain't nobody jumped you girl! Callie shot you a one," she shot back and turned to Mike. "They shot a one daddy!"

"Just like you about to," Mike declared and sat back to watch the action. He picked up his phone to capture the fight.

"I'm with the shits!" White girl Ki-ki declared and went for her clothes. Except Jersey girl was the shits so she wasn't waiting on her to get dressed. Ki-ki was bent over, pulling her panties back on when she got kicked in her face.

"Let me get jumped !"Jersey declared between pops and jabs.

"Oh, you wanna squirrel a bitch!" Ki-ki shouted and fought back. She unleashed a barrage of blows that left Jersey girl bloody and woozy. She was losing the fight and resorted to desperate measures.

"Unh!" she grunted and swung her razor. Ki-ki saw it coming but didn't have time to duck it. The best she could do was raise her hand to deflect the blade.

"Fuck! Fucking bitch!" Ki-ki shouted when her hand opened all the way across her palm. She grabbed a pillow from the bed to block the swipes and slashes. Blood poured from the open wound.

"A'ight, a'ight," Mike said when the room was beginning

to look like a crime scene. Jersey girl was still after her, forcing him to repeat himself. "I said a'ight!"

"Get her!" Ki-ki pleaded since Jersey was still after her. He let out a deep sigh as he stood from the bed. He threw a quick swing that connected with Jersey girl's jaw and dropped her the bad habit she was. Ki-ki wanted to kick the sleeping girl but Mike had other plans.

"Wrap that up so you can pack. Once you pack, get the fuck out and never come back!" he said over his shoulder as he walked out of the room.

"I need some money! Mike!" she called after him. A glance down at the sleeping girl reminded him of what kind of monster she was dealing with. She quickly gathered what she could and got up out of there.

"HOW'S IT COMING?" Dominique asked as she came into the studio. Three months had passed so the album should be near completion.

"Fine. OK. Mmhm," the girls replied from around the room.

"Depends on your definition of OK," Malik groaned. He got paid whether they were productive or not but he preferred to make music. These girls were doing everything but.

P-money spent more time going live with her growing number of followers. The P-hive was up another two million and begging for her to visit every state in the nation. Callie didn't have a C-hive but did have a boyfriend. And Zenobia, well she was high.

Z-money juggled her drug habit, relationship with Flash and at least showing up to every studio session on time. Lacrecia did her part and fucked him every chance she got. Which ironically helped their relationship since he didn't have to stray too far to quench his licentiousness. Instead of being seen with different women he discretely fucked her friend.

"Well, how many songs did you guys finish?" Dominique asked to cut around the excuses.

"Huh? Who? Ion know?" the girls guessed but Malik was keeping score.

"A total of four," he snitched.

"Nuh-uh! Six!" Callie insisted.

"No, one of them was wack so I deleted it. The other is a solo," he replied.

"The other three groups have completed their whole albums. Mixed, mastered and ready to go," Dominique huffed. They had a growing roster of hungry new artists but the stars were holding everything up.

"So," Penny pouted.

"The so, is that everyone is ready so we can go on tour. The Pretty Thugs, world tour! A ten million dollar tour!" she fussed since it meant a cool million for her.

"Well, we ain't got time to kick it now auntie!" Zenobia said on her way into the booth. Hearing the number was motivation to get it done.

"Word!" Callie concurred and followed.

"Sooner we get this done, the sooner I can do my solo joint," Penny muttered on the way in.

"Let me hear the beats y'all chose?" Dominique

demanded. She hand picked twelve more out of the twenty they agreed upon. "Now, let's get this done!"

"Where are you going then?" Callie wanted to know.

"Doctor appointment..." she said over her shoulder with a sinister smile and left them alone.

"Mmhm!" Callie laughed since the only doctor she was seeing was the one she was dating. Dominique showed him her vagina daily and he wasn't even a gynecologist. The money was enough motivation to bang out three more songs that day.

"Well, that's a wrap for the day," Callie decided. Penny rolled her eyes since she was growing tired of her deciding everything. She kept it to herself since she had plans for the night herself.

"Night you mean," Zenobia sang when she looked at her watch.

"Tryna get home to that man of yours huh?" Penny laughed. It was a slick remark since the man was a well known womanizer.

"Yup! Flash has been so patient!" she revealed. He didn't complain at all about the long days she spent in the studio. Most times he was already waiting at the house when she got in.

"That's love chica," Callie quickly shot back. This time it was her eyes who rolled at Penny. "You must have run out of batteries?"

"Actually, I have a date tonight," Penny sang and did a little twerk. Not that she didn't need batteries, because she did. Plus she had no intentions on fucking on this first date. However, if he got a second date it came with some pussy.

"Oh yeah, with Death Star!" Zenobia sang happily. She

saw the P-hive going crazy lately when he asked for a date after months of public flirting.

"Trap, Death Trap," Penny corrected and got a giggle out of Callie. "What's so funny?"

"Only trap that boy has seen is a mouse trap!" she replied and howled at her own joke. It was funny enough to get a laugh and head shake from Zenobia. Then again, she was pretty high so the ceiling fan could get a laugh out of her.

"And that's why he's still alive to talk about it," Penny snipped and took all the air out of the room. Even Malik went wide eyed at the dis. It could be taken a few different ways but none of them were good. Luckily there was no air left in the room, forcing Callie to take a breath before responding.

"Bruh, what's that supposed to mean?" she asked, tensed just like a mouse trap. If she was talking about Lil Bruh she had zero fucks to give. If she meant Voodoo, they were fighting.

"Nothing. Ion mean nothing," Penny decided and turned to leave. "I'll see y'all tomorrow."

"She ain't mean nothing by that!" Zenobia assured her even though she didn't know one way or another. She just wanted to keep the peace that kept the money flowing into her bank account. That kept the drugs flowing into her system and clothes into her closets.

"Yeah she did. Sis been on some bull shit. She's getting the big head," Callie growled as she still glared in the direction the girl just went.

"She good," her friend said and gathered her belongings to leave.

"Good hell! That chick said she should get twice as much

as us to go perform in them white ass states!" she informed.

"Ain't no such thing as a white state mama," Zenobia laughed.

"Uh, Wisconsin, Montana, Iowa..." Callie rattled off.

"Oh, yeah," her friend chuckled as they headed out to the car. "Them some white ass states but guess who album they buying? The Pretty Thugs! That's who! She can wait until her solo joint comes out cuz I ain't finna take no shorts!"

"Oh she came off the bullshit! And I got the same five million dollar offers as she got for my solo project!" Callie spat hotly and regretted instantly. Dominique had already confided that the offers for Z-money were much lower. The demand for C-money was as high as P, but Z was bringing up the rear.

"Five million!" Zenobia cheered and went wide eyed. She was spending money like water and five million would be right on time. Especially since they would all make at least that much off the second album and tour. Plus merchandising. "I'm finna buy Lil girl a car."

"Well, come to the dealership. I'll tell hubby to hook you up!" Callie cheered. Her free shoutouts and plugs generated so much business Ervin was preparing to open a second location.

"Hubby huh? OK then!" Zenobia laughed and cheered. They shared a hug before getting into their own vehicles.

"She gonna be a'ight!" Callie said to herself as she pulled away from her friend.

"Whew! Long overdue!" Zenobia exclaimed and whipped out a package of coke. Her friends noticed the difference when she snuck hits in the bathroom. So now she just waited until the sessions were over to get it in.

CHAPTER 11

"Hips like J-lo, lips like play dough, bow to the queen cuz I say so..." P-money rapped in the mirrored wall of the elevator as it descended.

She stopped abruptly when it stopped on a familiar floor. Even though she and Zenobia lived in the same building they rarely ran into each other. In fact they saw each other more in the studio across town than they did in the building. So it was purely coincidence when it opened on Zenobia and Flash headed out for a night on the town with Lacrecia in tow.

"Hey Penny!" Lacrecia sang and wrapped her up in a hug.

"Hey Lil sis!" Penny greeted happily. She may or may not be getting the big head but would never forget that the girl took a bullet for her.

"You look nice!" Lacrecia nodded when they broke off the embrace. She followed her social media too and recalled why, "That's right! You got a date with Death Trap!"

"Yes girl!" Penny replied while Zenobia bit her lip not to laugh. Callie had called him a light skin Vanilla Ice and it took everything she had not to laugh.

"Ooh guess what?" the teen cheered but couldn't contain herself long enough for a guess. Not that Penny intended to try. "Z and Flash buying me a car!"

"Word! OK then!"she cheered happily and looked over to the couple. "Hey Z!"

"Sup P. Yeah, she has been so helpful. Be babysitting my man while I am in the studio," she explained. Penny saw a flash of guilt on Flash's face as he looked down. Lacrecia didn't flinch so she dismissed it. "She needs her own whip."

"She does. Let's go thirds," Penny offered out of loyalty.

"Bet that," Zenobia asked as the door opened to the parking level. They said their 'see you laters' and went their separate ways.

Penny knew to drive her own car to the date so she would be free to leave whenever she felt like it. She hoped to have a good time so she suggested bowling. That would give the P-hive something to cheer at when she went live.

"Hmp..." she huffed at the Bentley Zenobia just got in and decided she wanted one too. A better thought came to mind when she arrived at the bowling alley and saw a pearl white Rolls Royce sitting regally out front. A black one pulled next to her as she parked, "Must be a sign!"

"Hey there," Death Trap greeted and flashed a diamond studded smile that cost as much as a family home. He was a pretty six footer with light brown coils of hair courtesy of his mix of races.

"Hey ya self cutie," she laughed as they leaned in for a hug. Fans of both snapped pics and videos that would be uploaded before they got inside. They posed for a few more and signed a few autographs before heading inside.

"You wanna see my dick?" he asked out of the clear blue.

"Huh?" she reeled and wondered if she heard correctly. She did, and cracked up. "I already saw, but thanks."

"There's that smile I fell in love with!" he pointed as she grinned and blushed just like he planned.

"Yeah, I like you," she nodded as they went to their booth. Both heads turned to the lively lane and saw another rapper holding court with his crew.

"Pussy ass nigga!" Death Trap muttered. He made sure to say it under his breath so dude wouldn't hear it though.

"Who?" Penny reeled and looked past the rapper to see who he was referring to. People say a lot about dude but, pussy ass nigga wasn't any of them.

"Doobie fuck ass Daddie. Nigga gonna cop the same whip I bought!" he lied. The truth was he was copying Doobie since he was the hottest rapper in the country. Death Trap saw Doobie post a picture in his Rolls and rushed out to buy one too.

"Yeah, well let's bowl," she offered to change the subject. She liked him but Doobie was her friend.

"Let's!" he agreed. They both went live and put on for their legions of fans as they alternated between gutter balls and strikes.

They got along great and were having a great time but this was also a great publicity move. Their lives had nearly a million people watching from around the globe. Their followers swapped and both gained a hundred thousand followers by the time they finished up.

"P muhfuckin money!" Doobie Daddie greeted on his

way by. His girl Taylor rolled her eyes when he walked over
to greet her.

"Oh hey Doobie!" she sang and vacillated on whether or
not to hug him since her date was hating on him. Doobie
took the option away when he leaned in for a side hug to be
respectful of his woman.

"Hold the fuck up bro!" Death Trap protested.

"Chill, I'm just saying hello," Penny pleaded and was set
to leave.

"Nah, this nigga tried me up!" he insisted and went live
again to show off in front of his followers.

"Bro?" Doobie laughed and shook his head. He reached
for his girl's hand again and turned to leave.

"Yeah, better take your bitch ass on!" the man called after
him and stopped him in his tracks.

"Can you make it quick please," Taylor requested since
even she knew that had to be checked.

"Un-uh! He doesn't mean nothing," Penny pleaded and
got in between the two men. Doobie wasn't going to go
through her so he fell back.

"Thank you," Doobie's girl was saying but Death Trap
ran up and took a swing at him.

"Did he just hit me?" Doobie asked his girl of the
light tap.

"Nah, he did," she informed as he tried to squirrel him
again. Except Doobie dipped this one and came up with a
few of his own.

'Pap, pap, pap-pap, pap' and the fight was over. Doobie
Daddie grabbed his girl's hand and continued on out of the
club.

"Shit!" Penny fussed as she looked down and her date

sleeping on the floor. It got worse when she noticed his phone propped to catch the action. All she could do was turn it off and curse some more. "Shit!"

"What happened?" Death Trap asked when he came to.

"Nothing. Let's go," she sighed and helped him up. "I'll drive."

"OK cuz, I'm sleepy," he said as she helped him to the car.

"Let me get this," she said and pulled the fob from his hand. She wanted to see what the Rolls drove like anyway. "Oh yeah! I'm getting one of these hoes!"

"Hoes," the man repeated from the passenger seat as they rode. She just shook her head and wondered how this would play out. She deleted the video but thousands had seen it. She clicked over to Doobie's page to see he was live.

"Y'all don't trip that shit. Me and my nigga Death Trap just played a hoax on his girl P-muhfuckin-money..." he laughed magnanimously and dismissed the whole incident.

'Ha ha! Not funny! I'ma get y'all back for that' she typed and added to show. That Doobie Daddie was a hell of guy, just like his pops.

"WHAT THE HECK..." Death Trap asked when he awoke to the smell of food cooking. He had lived in the mansion for a few months and never cooked a single meal. Plus he was fully dressed and strained to recall how he got home. Something about the bowling alley came to mind, "The heck?"

"Breakfast is the heck!" Penny announced and came in with a tray full of food for him and her.

"I got into a fight?" he asked and felt the knots on his forehead.

"Not a real one," she repeated since that's the narrative they were going with. "A hoax."

"Oh yeah." he nodded and agreed like he remembered. Unfortunately he was a pill head too and sometimes whole days disappeared from his memory banks. "You cooked!"

"I cooked," she repeated happily. She was quite proud of herself as well since she didn't cook often. Besides, the run to the store allowed her to drive the fancy car again.

She went live and announced to the P-hive that P-money was copping a Rolls today. Her accountant called immediately to make sure she leased, not bought the nearly half a million dollar car. Unlike Death Trap who paid cash for his. He didn't mind making major purchases like that since the cash was flooding in from every direction. With so much airplay he made money every second, of every day. Penny had referred this same money manager to her friends but Callie went with the one Jovita recommended, while Zenobia, 'wasn't stutting that shit'.

Zenobia woke up to an erection pressed against her back side so she did the reasonable thing and lifted her leg. Flash did the responsible thing and reached for a rubber so she wouldn't have a fit. He had yet to use one with Lacrecia even though he fucked her as much as he did his woman.

"Let me..." she changed her mind and positions by rolling him onto his back. She mounted him and reached back to guide him inside.

Flash was hit or miss when he did the driving but she always climaxed when she took the wheel. He gripped her yellow ass cheeks and held on while she rode off in search of a nut. It was right around the corner and didn't take long to find. Luckily for him, she shivered, shook and contracted so hard that when she came she drug him along with her.

"Argh!" he grunted and filled the condom up. Lacrecia, who had been listening at the door, twisted her lips and rolled her eyes. In a stroke of pure audacity she actually felt some kind of way about Zenobia fucking her own man.

It was getting so good to Flash that he offered to buy her a car just before Zenobia came in yesterday with the idea. Then Penny offered to go in on the vehicle as well. Once they started their day off with a nut, they showered dressed and got ready to go buy lil girl her first car.

"Y'ALL NEED to give me a commission!" Callie huffed as she sat on her boyfriend's desk. She may have been a star and all that but loved hanging out at the dealership with Ervin.

"I just gave you a tip this morning," he reminded.

"That was more than just the tip mister!" she announced loud enough to make his employees blush.

Ervin had pulled a few car up front for P-money to pick from when she arrived. A nice selection of Beemers and Benzes sat in a shiny row for lil girl to pick from. They were the first to arrive in the Bentley so they headed out to greet them.

"Hey girl!" Callie sang and threw her arms open. Lacrecia took off and came over to embrace her.

"Hey C-money!" she sang as they hugged. She looked Ervin up and down over her shoulder as they did.

"Sup Callie," Zenobia sang and hugged her next.

"Hey girl," she replied. "Pick a ride so I can get a tip!"

"I know you better be giving my girl more than just the tip!" Zenobia fussed at Ervin.

"You better believe it!" he laughed and embraced her before shaking Flash's hand. "Nice game the other night!"

"What! Brooklyn killed us!" Flash grimaced.

"That's what I mean. I'm a Brooklyn fan," he laughed. The two men stepped aside and talked sports while the women shopped for a car.

"Which one can I get?" Lacrecia whined unsurely. Some of these cars cost more than the house she grew up in.

"OK, turn that way," Zenobia began and turned her in the direction of the five figure cars. "Now, anything you want!"

"You stooopid!" Callie laughed at the exchange. "Where P at?"

"Ion know? She said she was buying a Rolls today. And she knew we were coming here to get her a car," Zenobia replied. She checked P-money's page and saw she just posted her daily pic for her sponsors. Something Penny and Callie did religiously since it paid them. Zenobia wore whatever she wanted and rarely posted much anymore. Except when Jovita would jump down her throat and make her.

"Well, bae set out some heat for her to pick from," Callie said proudly and pointed at the row of half a million dollar cars in different colors. The triple black Wraith actually made her a little moist when she first saw it.

"This one?" Lacrecia asked timidly and pointed at a convertible Jaguar. The ten year old car looked a lot more expensive than it actually cost.

"Or that one, or that one!" Zenobia declared and pointed

down the line of trade ins. The dealership had a thriving market for rich men's side chicks and baby mamas. The older luxury cars usually kept them side-chicking and baby mama-ing.

"This one!" she decided and slid inside of a convertible BMW. She gripped the wheel firmly and looked straight ahead so she wouldn't see anything that would change her mind.

"I'll tell him," Callie said and went to find her man. She found him talking Flash into the white Rolls.

"Let me see where this chile is..." Zenobia said and checked Penny's page since it was more accurate than a call or a text. Her eyes went wide when she saw what she saw so she clicked away.

"See how she drives..." Ervin said and tossed her the keys. He frowned up at the look she gave Flash before getting behind the wheel. He looked at Flash to see if he saw it and saw him shoot a quick wink.

"P-money going live," Callie said when she pulled out her phone to call the girl and saw the notification. She decided to just join in and say what she had to say in real time.

"Sup P-hive! This yo girl P to the MF money! I told y'all I'm finna cop me a Rolls, so I'm at Stuart exotic cars in Buck-head..." Penny said and spun to show the lot.

"Wow," Callie gasped. She wasn't quite sure what to feel or say. It wasn't exactly a betrayal since she didn't have to shop with her man. Nor did she actually say she was coming here to cop the new car.

"What's wrong babe? You're pale!" Ervin asked and looked around to see if he could see what had made his woman so flustered so suddenly.

"I'm sorry baby. Penny went up the block to buy the car," she sighed. It bothered her to have him pull out the expensive cars from the showroom floor.

"It's all good. Trust me, Stuart needs all the help they can get. Another slow month and I'm buying them out for a second location," he shrugged and headed back over to talk to Flash.

"Work it baby," Callie laughed when she saw Ervin hand him the keys to the white Rolls. Flash hopped in for a ride as Lacrecia returned.

"Ooh girl, this is it!" the girl cheered.

"It's yours then," Zenobia said and took her inside to handle the paperwork.

"I got something on it too!" Callie called after them. Splitting the twenty thousand dollar car four ways cost less than they made in an hour.

"Sold!" Flash cheered when he returned in the Rolls. He too went inside to handle the paperwork. His Bentley made a nice trade for the upgrade.

"Babe..." Ervin called and tossed something to Callie. She snatched it out midair and scrunched her face at it.

"What do you want me to do with this?" she asked of the key fob she just caught.

"Make it look good. It's yours," he replied and walked off.

"Let me find out..." she said and pressed a button on the fob. The black Wraith flashed its blacked out lights in reply. "Welp, looks like someone getting some head when he gets off."

CHAPTER 12

"Yeah bitch!" Callie cheered at her perfect timing. Penny was pulling into the parking lot just ahead of her in her new car.

They both pulled into the spots reserved for the room they were booked in. The spots were extra wide to accommodate the luxury vehicles of the affluent patrons. Penny pulled in and pulled down the mirror to check herself again. Nothing had changed since the last check a few red lights ago so she stepped out. Right as Callie stepped out of new Rolls. Her eyes nearly popped out of her head but she quickly recovered.

"Nuh-uh! Girl that shit is fierce!" she cheered and walked around the car.

"Yours is too!" Callie replied and looked hers over as well. It was all that, but she liked her own better. "My man gave it to me."

"Shit! I totally didn't even think to go to his dealership!"

she reeled and appeared genuine. "Death Trap just referred me to where he copped his."

"Word," Callie nodded at the plausible explanation. She would accept it so they headed inside. Both noticed Zenobia's empty parking spot but neither spoke on it. She had been doing much better lately and had yet to miss or even be late for a session. Both hoped this wasn't the start.

"Hey bitches!" Zenobia laughed when her friend's eyes went wide to find she was there first.

"OK then!" Callie cheered and nodded in approval.

"My bish!" Penny laughed and dapped her up.

"Well, I think one more will get it?" Malik asked. The door opened and Jovita and Dominique walked in on the question.

"We can go one more," Jovita agreed. She had just heard the completed songs and agreed, "You killed that sophomore jinx. This album is hotter than the first!"

"It is," Dominique agreed. "I wish y'all got it done quicker tho. Jersey girl just released her new single."

"That diss track huh?" Callie guessed correctly since both heads nodded.

"That bitch don't quit!" Penny fussed and grimaced.

"That bitch ass nigga don't give up," Jovita corrected since Mike was behind it. All eyes went wide hearing that come out of her mouth.

"Man, fuck that bum hoe," Callie protested. "I'm making more off ads from the video of me beating that ass than she made off they whole album!"

"Facts!" Penny cheered since she got richer by the day.

"Oh! Yeah, I looked that contract over for Tiffany," Jovita

remembered. Zenobia had asked for the favor to help the girl get some money from Mike.

"And?" she asked hopefully. Zenobia had threw her some money to get by but it would be great for Tiffany to get paid.

"And she dead. I'm not sure if they can't read, or didn't read, or just didn't understand. Because that contract was shit! They pretty much signed away all rights to everything," Zenobia winced. The deal was so lopsided it was as hard to read as watching a rape. Because that's exactly what it amounted to. A financial rape. "Plus, they didn't write a single word on the whole album. So no publishing checks. Dude probably netted ten million off them."

"Dang!" Zenobia reeled since she was still in shock about the fat publishing checks they had coming. She had already spent hers in her mind.

"Dang is right. All they had coming was peanuts but it doesn't look like they even got that," Jovita said, shaking her head.

"Well, she got nutted in!" Penny laughed. "At least she can get child support!"

"Hmp!" both Callie and Dominique huffed since they thought alike. If it were up to them Tiffany's baby would have an inheritance coming.

"Speaking of the IRS," Jovita recalled, even though no one said anything about the IRS. She had just paid a chunk of business and personal taxes and wanted to make sure they handled their personal business.

"Man fuck them folks!" Callie pouted like she wanted to cry. She even had her boyfriend's accountant double check hers and the amount still wanted to make her cry. She was too tough to cry so she just cursed instead. "Bunch of bitches!"

"I know right!" Penny fussed since she had to pay out even more than Callie did since she made more money. Everyone murmured and moped about taxes except Zenobia.

"Huh? What?" she asked when all eyes turned in her direction.

"Girl, I hope you're keeping up with your business!" Dominique fussed like an auntie.

"Did you reach out to the firm I gave you guys?" Jovita asked. She certainly had too much to worry about with a whole company and growing roster than her taxes.

"No, I'ma use Flash folks," she replied. The future tense meant she hadn't done anything yet. Except spend so much money she couldn't guess the amount. Luckily the flood gates were still wide open and money was flowing in from every direction.

"YOU LOOK NICE!" Callie gushed when her man came out of the bedroom in a tailored suit.

"You don't!" he reeled and frowned up. "The fuck you got on?"

"Uh, it's called high fashion sir. It's our album release party, I have to look good!" she shot back. The tiny dress was completely transparent so he could clearly see she wasn't wearing a lick of underclothes. Not to mention the dip in the neckline was below her navel.

"Well, high fashion your ass back into the room and find

something that shows your man ain't a pimp or a simp! The fuck!" he snapped.

"But I..." Callie was saying but a titty fell out.

"Nigga..." Ervin began but Callie cracked up at her joke. No way would she wear anything like this out of the house even if she didn't have a man. Even if it wasn't a joke she didn't mind being checked about her attire. She had a whole man because only a simp, wimp or pimp would let his woman go out in public looking like a prostitute.

The black men and women of the civil rights era wore suits and dresses, daily. They were well groomed, sober, articulate and educated. Somewhere, some how along the way black folks got it fucked up. Their grand and great grand parents didn't get hosed down by fire hoses, bit by dogs and heads busted for this current generation to dress like prostitutes or clowns.

"This chick tried me up!" Ervin grumbled to himself as Callie changed into the real outfit for the night. She heard him and literally howled with laughter.

"My bad baby," she cooed and posed for him. The dress was form fitting, yet tasteful. Plus it was the same hue of blue as his suit, which was intentional.

"Just keep that same energy when I get my lick back," he nodded. "You looked beautiful!"

"You do too," she admitted and they had a moment.

"I assume you're driving?" he asked since she drove the Rolls every chance she got.

"You can drive, my car," she snickered. His electric Audi was a work of art but her Wraith was, well, a Wraith.

"Gee, thanks," he said and took the keys. He was a

gentleman so he opened and closed all doors until she was safely seated in her car.

"I need to either look for a new place or sign a new lease soon," Callie remarked as they rode. She expected his usual moment of silence to process like he did with most things.

"No you don't," he said immediately of both options and kept on driving. Now it was her turn to process since she never stayed at the old apartment anyway. Her hand reached over and took his free hand for the rest of the ride. She gave it a squeeze to accept the offer to live with him. Nothing had to change since she practically lived there already.

"WHERE YOU AT!" Zenobia fussed when she took Flash's call.

"Landing in a few," he said from the phone on the plane.

"Well, come straight to the venue as soon as you land. We have to go!" she whined.

"Want me to pick him up?" Lacrecia offered since she heard one side of the conversation.

"Would you?" Zenobia asked but didn't wait for an answer. She shouldn't have to since it was the labor that paid for the free ride she was getting.

"Hell yeah!" she shot back. Flash had been on a two week road trip with the team and she missed him just as much as Zenobia did.

"OK baby, she is coming to pick you up. Love you too. Bye," she said and clicked off. "How do I look?"

"Like a damn super star!" Lacrecia declared. One because it was true in the Gucci tube dress. Even though the company didn't comp her no matter how many 'likes' she got. The other brands did but she rarely wore them. Second, Lacrecia said it because it paid the bills, put money in her designer purse and designer labels on her fast ass.

"You looking good yourself chica!" she admitted. Lacrecia had filled out quite nicely and filled her short skirt out as well.

"Thank you!" she cooed and followed her out of the condo. She suddenly stopped and rushed back to her room, but was back in a flash.

"You forgot something?" Zenobia asked when she came back.

"Huh? No, I'm good," she replied since she only removed her panties. Zenobia could only laugh and shake her head at her little friend who had become the sister she never had.

"Love you lil girl!" she assured as they waited for the elevator.

"I love you too sis!" she squealed and hugged her tightly. The elevator door dinged open while they embraced.

"Awe!" Penny moaned and stuck her lip out when she saw the touching scene. She couldn't help but come and get her some too.

"Awe!" Death Trap seconded the special moment. He and Penny had been hanging tough over the last few months. She hadn't fucked him yet but it was definitely good for her brand. She absorbed more of his ten million followers every day.

"Oh hey DT," Zenobia greeted. She only used his initials since the name always reminded her of Callie's dis and made her laugh. He did manage to save face after getting beat up since he went with the whole prank narrative.

"You ladies look nice! Ready for tonight?" he asked them both as if Lacrecia were a part of the act.

"Thank you! Yes!" they sang as they descended to the parking level.

"See y'all there," Penny said and headed to the matching Rolls Royces. She was in diva mode so she let him drive.

"Want me to take my own car?" Lacrecia asked, then explained. "Since I gotta go to the airport."

"Hell yeah. My baby said she don't like no one else pushing her," Zenobia said of her new Bentley. They both hopped in their vehicles and dropped their tops.

Halfway to the club Flash called back to say they were landing. Zenobia relayed the message and Lacrecia peeled off from her bumper and headed towards the airport. Good thing she removed her panties because she got a little moist from anticipation.

A line of cars, SUVs and limos were pulled up to the private hangar the team jet uses. Lacrecia was familiar with it since she accompanied Zenobia a few times from other road trips. Flash stepped out and looked around until he spotted her. A smile spread on his face as he made his way over.

"Hey there!" he greeted and sat in the passenger seat. She had already moved it all the way back to accommodate his long legs.

"Hey yourself," she replied as he looked around. There were no paparazzi present so he leaned over and twirled his tongue inside her mouth. The thick thighs couldn't be ignored so he squeezed one. Somehow his hand made its way up her legs and found her juicy, young box.

"Fuck!" he swore when she soaked his fingers.

"She missed you!" she laughed and pulled away. "Did y'all win?"

"I play for the Hawks, of course not!" he laughed. He didn't need to give any directions when he pulled his phone to make a call.

"Hello!" Zenobia shouted over the music.

"I'm on the way! Be there in a few!" he said loud enough to be heard by passing cars but she couldn't make it out.

"You landed? Huh?" they shouted back and forth. "Just text it!"

"Flash?" Callie asked when Zenobia smiled at the incoming text. Which reminded her that she forgot her own phone. "Shit!"

"What?" Zenobia asked as she stood.

"Forgot my phone," she replied and tried to squeeze past her man. Her head shook since the valet took the car away.

"Like I would really let you walk two blocks to the lot," Ervin sighed and set off to retrieve her phone.

"We got us some good men!" Zenobia cheered. Callie cheesed and nodded. Voodoo may have been her first love but this was real love. Ervin treated her in ways the thug would never have been able to. They both looked up and saw Penny and Death Trap approaching and schmoozing their way through the crowd. Z saw the smirk on Callie's face and said, "Don't start!"

"I ain't say nothing!" she shot back innocently. "I like Mouse Trap!"

"See!" Zenobia howled. Women can be so phony so they both stood and smiled to receive their girl.

"Hey!" they sang and Penny sang, "Hey!"

Death Trap just smiled as if he hadn't heard Penny

griping the whole way over how she couldn't wait to go solo. The other girls were riding off her hype. She was the biggest draw, etc. The only thing she couldn't say was she was the best rapper in the group. That distinction clearly went to Callie. Whose man just happened to reach the parking lot.

"Huh?" Ervin asked when he saw a convertible in the back of the lot. There were plenty of drop tops in the valet lot but this was the only one with the top down. Not a good idea in this or any other city since crack heads will steal the stink off shit, then try to sell it.

He would have minded his business if the car didn't look so familiar. A closer look showed the Clayton MotorSports plate that went on every car he sold. That meant this was the same car he just sold to his girlfriend's girlfriend, which made it her business. He headed over but a moan stopped him in his tracks. It was the hiss that followed that made him continue, with his nosey ass.

Sometimes being nosey can get you more than you bargained for. Even without looking at his watch, this was one of them some times. His eyes went wide when he got a glimpse of the face leaned back in the passenger seat. He had just left Flash's girl inside so he had to get a peek at who was riding the dick vigorously enough to hear the coochie splash from feet away. He didn't want to walk up on the car so he walked around. He nearly didn't recognize Lacrecia since she obviously wasn't wearing a fuck face when they met at his dealership.

"I'm finna cum!" she whined and did just that.

"Shit! Me, too!" Flash grunted and let one go inside the young girl. Ervin had seen more than enough and slinked back to the club.

"What's wrong babe!" Callie shrieked in near panic when she saw the look on his face.

"Who?" Ervin asked defensively.

"You are so strange," Callie laughed and reached for her phone. "Let me see my phone."

"Shit!" he fussed when he realized he totally forgot what he went to get.

"Never mind baby," she cooed since he seemed so confused. He was even more confused when Flash and Lacrecia came over happily. Flash smiled, hugged and greeted his woman like he hadn't just fucked her friend, real good.

CHAPTER 13

"Hey baby!" Zenobia cooed, kissed and fawned over her man like a woman should when he returns from getting drug in different NBA stadiums.

"Hey yourself!" he said and shoved his tongue down her throat. They huddled up in the booth to catch up. Ervin tilted his head curiously at the spectacle. He liked Flash up to that point but now had no respect for the man. If a man's wife or girlfriend can't trust him, no one should.

"Hey ladies!" Jovita sang as she came over trailed by the other new artist on the roster. Bama, Lizzet and a set of twin girls called Frick and Frack. They were all making noise in the industry but the Pretty Thugs were the stars of the show. That's why they were all featured on the new album for exposure.

"Hey y'all!" Penny cheered from her perch on Death Trap's lap. "Y'all ready for this tour?"

"Yeah!" they all cheered and clapped. Lizzet took it step further and twerked her three hundred pound ass cheeks.

The big girl was an advocate that big girls can do anything smaller girls can. Which, they obviously can. Should they, is the question.

"Yeah, I'ma need you to take that over there," Callie said, like Callie says. Not only did she not want anyone twerking in front of her man, she was worried about what that twerk wind might smell like.

"You guys get ready," Dominique directed since they were all performing before the DJ played the new Thugs album.

Radio, video, streaming and retail were all present for a glimpse of the plate they would all eat off. They were all still eating good from the first album. So this was exciting for all. There were also a few ravenous record execs looping around like hyenas, hoping for a bite.

"Nice turn out!" Mike said from behind Dominique, who spun like she was ready to fight.

"What do you want? Cuz, I know you want something!" she snapped and alerted her date.

"Everything OK dear?" her doctor boyfriend wanted to know.

"Yes Carl. Just business," she assured him with a reassuring pat on his chest.

"Yeah, I used to give her the business," Mike laughed wickedly. "Have her do that thing with her tongue."

"Bruh..." the doctor began to snap but Dominique stepped in before he went too far. The good doctor saved lives, Mike took them.

"Do I need to call security? This is the album release party for our group! What do you want?" she demanded as she stood between the glaring men.

"Just paying respects. Congrats," he nodded and stepped away to watch the show.

"Ex?" Doctor Carl asked even though he was smart enough to ascertain for himself.

"Biggest mistake of my life," she replied as she squinted at the man. For the life of her she couldn't recall what she ever saw in the man.

"You bounced back quite nicely," he said of himself and got a kiss for the right answer.

"I did," she agreed but kept an eye on Mike. He was up to something, she wanted to find out what.

"THAT'S A FUCKING BANGER!" Death Trap cheered when the last song of the new album played. The girl's maturity as artist and women was evident in their follow-up album. It was even better than the first.

"Thank you!" Penny squealed and hugged him tightly. They pulled back enough to look at each, then back in for a kiss. The make believe couple had shared pecks and hugs for the cameras but this make out wasn't make believe. Callie nudged Zenobia and nodded towards the couple looking like a couple.

"Dang!" Zenobia sang when they didn't come up for air. Meanwhile, Ervin just glared at Flash like he had two heads.

"Well, two days and were off for four months!" Jovita announced. Negotiations for a world tour were also in the works. The Pretty Thugs world tour would net more millions for everyone.

"Yay," Ervin quipped sarcastically at the news he already

knew. Since he already knew the strain of a long distance relationship. They were just getting to know each other last time they were on the road. This time they were living together.

"Awe," Callie pouted and felt his pain. She didn't want to leave him anymore than he did. "We'll work it out."

"You gonna behave yourself while I'm gone?" Zenobia dared and cocked her head at Flash. She had to admit he was doing better than before since he hadn't been linked to any strange women since they began dating.

"Of course!" he replied adamantly.

"Don't worry, I'ma keep him straight!" Lacrecia vowed.

"You're gonna be with us lil mama!" Zenobia corrected. "Gotta earn yo keep shawty."

"Bae..." Callie laughed and tapped Ervin's leg since he was staring at them.

"Huh? Yeah," he replied and shook it off. He wasn't sure how to handle what he just saw. This could distract the whole group and ruin the tour. Ultimately his shoulders shrugged with the fact that it wasn't his business. Penny and Death Trap stole everyone's attention when they rushed for the door.

"Looks like that public farce about to go private," Dominique guessed when she saw that glint in Penny's eyes. She knew it well since she had one in hers. She dragged her man out the door as well.

"Thank you," Penny said when Death Trap joined her in the front seat after opening and closing her door like a gentleman should.

"You can thank me when we get to your spot," he offered and wiggled his eyebrows suggestively.

"Or, I can thank you now..." she replied and reached over to rub his crotch. Then pulled the zipper down and removed the dick.

"Mmmm!" he moaned when the heat of her mouth engulfed the tip of his dick. It only got wetter and better as she inched his inches down her throat.

'Gawk' escaped when she ran out of mouth before he ran out of dick. Next was that white girl magic when she worked her wrist, lips and tongue with the synchronization of a Swiss watch. And that's pretty damn good if you don't know.

"Fuck," he replied as he fought to keep the car going straight. His legs began shifting beneath him and Penny threw it into overdrive. He was on the verge of an explosion just before she snatched him free from her mouth. "Shit!"

"Yeah baby!" she cooed and stroked his dick. She made sure to aim the barrel away from her expensive dress. Good thing too because the first pulse plastered the driver side window. The next blast hit the steering wheel. The rest gave his dry cleaner some extra work.

"Fuck!" he shouted because bomb head makes dude shout, fuck.

"And you better fuck me right!" she demanded as they reached her building. He parked haphazardly and rushed around to open her door. They made out hot and heavy on the elevator ride up to her unit. Penny lifted a leg to let him play in her pussy as they ascended. Sounds of her squishy box filled the quiet elevator.

They stumbled out the elevator and down the hall, still making out the entire way. She managed to open the door and they fell inside. Death Trap scooped her up and caveman carried her to her bedroom. She giggled when he tossed her on the bed.

"Uh, what are you doing?" Penny asked when he turned on the camera on his phone.

"Letting you film me eating your pussy," he said and handed her the phone. She checked to make sure he wasn't going live because she didn't want to be on a sex tape. Her career was doing well enough at the moment so it was too soon.

"Oh, ok," she agreed since her face wouldn't be on the video. She spread her legs wide as he leaned in for a lick. Then went for the kill. His twirling tongue threatened to make her throw her rose out the window. They made eye contact through the lens and screen as an intense orgasm began creeping through her soul.

"Mmhm," Death Trap hummed happily when she bust a nut in his mouth. She may not swallow on the first date but he didn't mind. It was a gusher too since she was overdue for some human contact. He clamped his lips over hers while she writhed around from the electric currents shooting through her body. As soon as they subsided he picked up the pace again and went for seconds.

"OK! OK!" Penny tapped after a second nut. "I need some dick now!"

"I got some dick!" he laughed and sat up. Her eyes were on his award winning dick while he took his phone back. He turned off the screen and sat it on her nightstand at the perfect angle to catch the good fucking he planned to give her.

"Hope you know what to do with it..." she said and twisted her lips. Some perfectly good dicks went to waste on dudes who didn't know how to use them. He just smirked as he secured the condom since she was about to find out for herself.

"OK then!" Death Trap cheered when it took some work to get inside of her. He fucked a few celebrity chicks and found most of them had been pretty thoroughly ran through. Not P-money though because she was, "So right, so tight!"

"And you sir, are rocking it, right!" she declared. And rock it right he did until she came again. Then flipped her into the next position for the next nut. "OK, OK, I'm good!"

"Nuh-uh," he laughed and flipped her into the next positive. He took total control even with her on top. He angled her just right and worked his hips up and down, in and out until she bust another nut. He joined her this time and filled his condom to the rim. They cuddled up and basked in afterglow of good sex and contemplated what came next.

"I see I'ma have to fuck someone up over this dick huh?" Penny asked only half seriously. If she learned anything from Zenobia it was not to snort coke in elevators and rappers have hoes. Lots and lots of hoes. So many hoes, they need a hoe phone to separate hoes from bros.

"I was just thinking the same thing," he sighed.

"About fucking someone up over the dick?" she snickered.

"Naw, about you," he confessed.

"OK, first. Ion be fucking like that. And two, you do," she reminded. "Plus you finna go on a world tour! You gonna be fucking Yugoslavian bitches. Vietnamese, um Cambodian..."

"You should come with me then," he offered. He didn't deny it because it was true. Everyone loves some Yugoslavian pussy but he wouldn't need it if she was with him.

"And blow off my own tour?" she huffed and rolled her eyes at the thought.

"Girl you would make ten times what you will make stateside!" he revealed.

"What, y'all must charge for shipping!" she quipped and giggled even though her curiosity was piqued.

"I guess you could say that?" he wondered. What he was sure of was they paid a premium for premium acts. He once made a cool million to do one show for some Arab prince's birthday. "Make that twenty times if you were solo."

"Hmp!" Penny huffed since she was just biding her time until that could happen. She had half of her solo album written and a slew of commitments from A list acts to appear. For the first time she looked at her girls like they were holding her back.

"A joint tour would kill," he put out there and closed his eyes. Penny heard his snores but her eyes didn't close. Not yet anyway because she had too much on her mind.

CHAPTER 14

The Pretty Thugs opened their national tour in their home city of Atlanta. Second and third shows had to be added when they sold out in minutes. The same thing was happening around the country once their lead single shot up the charts like a bullet.

Their status wasn't the only thing to change since their rider had quadrupled. Private jets ferried them between cities while other acts rode the bus with the equipment and help. It was the dues to fill the shoes since it cost to be the boss

. Not to mention they now required three separate suites instead of sharing one. There was no more shared crossing room and each diva required her own. Penny had even requested a private jet of her own until they told her it would come out of her pay. She changed her mind and chose to add that million to the millions in her growing bank account.

Callie flew back to Atlanta any time she could. Ervin met her in a few cities as well. Zenobia made sure her suite contained her drugs of choice at each stop. She and Lacrecia partied hard in each city. They crossed paths with Flash in Memphis since his team had a game there. Flash booked a sky box for the group but only two thirds showed up.

"Where's P-money?" Ervin asked since he always got a kick out of the colorful white girl.

"At some event," Callie answered and rolled her eyes. A white sorority house paid her twenty thousand dollars to appear at their house. The smart girl was smart enough to donate it back to the house and earn even more supporters.

"Yay baby!" Zenobia cheered when Flash made another three pointer. He was having a great game but his team lost another one in the end.

"Awe man!" Lacrecia moaned and Ervin twisted his lips.

"What?" Callie wanted to know. She noticed he got uncomfortable anytime he was around Lacrecia or Flash.

"Who? Nah, me?" he asked, confirming her suspicion. What he wasn't going to do was tell her about what he saw and heard because that moan was just like the one when she was riding Flash's dick in the parking lot.

"Mmhm," she hummed and squinted at him. The buzzer sounded and ended another blow out.

"At least my baby got his numbers!" Zenobia declared. She texted the triple double to her daddy who was also a Flash fan. She even took him to a visit before leaving for tour.

"He needs to go to New York!" Callie suggested and explained, "The Hawks suck!"

They chatted it up while Flash showered, changed and joined them in the sky box so they could convert the arena for tonight's concert.

"Hey baby!" Flash cheered when he entered the swank room. Ervin watched curiously to see both women's reaction.

"Good game baby!" Zenobia gushed and rushed him at the door. Ervin was the only one who saw Lacrecia roll her eyes when he scooped her up and shoved his tongue down her throat.

"Un-uh player! She gotta perform in a few hours!" Callie fussed playfully. "Gonna choke her to death with your dang tongue!"

"That's not what I'ma choke her with!" Flash laughed. The remark got a pop from Zenobia and another eye roll from Lacrecia.

A knock on the door alerted them to the arrival of the food. Drinks were already flowing from the in house bar but Flash took the liberty of ordering from one of Memphis's finest restaurants. They ate, talked and laughed while the stage and props were set up for tonight's show.

"Hmp!" Callie huffed when the elaborate harnesses were set up for P-money to fly down to the stage. Another would lower Z-money from the rafters but C-money preferred to walk on stage the old fashioned way.

"I know right," Zenobia laughed for the same reason. Penny was changing by the day but making a hundred grand a day will do that to a person. The other thugs were far behind since money was pouring in from every angle. Lacrecia was getting a little stank attitude herself lately but knew she had to control it, for now.

"Welp..." Callie sighed when the first fans started filing into the arena. It wouldn't be long before the local opening acts took the stage. They would be followed by the acts from the label, and finally the stars of the show.

"Yup, let's do this," Zenobia agreed and stood. That got yet another eye roll from the girl as they all headed to their separate dressing rooms.

Ervin and Callie talked business and scouted locations for future dealerships. They were equally yoked when it came to making their dollars make more dollars. Music was a goldmine but Callie knew it wouldn't last forever. Nor did she want it to since there was so much more to life. Plus, it wasn't as fun anymore anytime she had to leave her man. The frequent travel only made her want to travel more, but not for work. Earth was a big planet and she wanted to see more of it.

"Dang greedy!" Zenobia chided when Flash inhaled six of the lines of cocaine in succession.

"Ugh!" he reeled and grimaced like Tony Montana sniffing a mountain of coke off his desk. "There's plenty more where that came from!"

"I see!" she cheered when he dumped more coke onto the table. Zenobia passed Lacrecia the blunt and leaned in for a line. Lacrecia and Flash shared a glance and blew kisses while her head was down.

"Slow down baby! You have to perform!" Flash reminded when Zenobia repeated what he just did.

"Shit, you do too sir," she shot back. She didn't want a repeat of limp dick Pretty Boy.

"Oh I'ma be good all night! I took my Viagra and I got a lil of this..." he said and produced a smaller bag of browner powder.

"Oooh I want some!" Lacrecia begged and bounced.

"You don't even know what it is!" Zenobia laughed, then turned to Flash and asked, "What is it?"

"H, that boy oh boy," he said and took a tiny hit with the tip of his finger nail. He put the tip of his finger back in just enough to allow a few grains to adhere. "Here."

Zenobia leaned in and touched her tongue to it. Her face scrunched from the bitter taste but that didn't dissuade Lacrecia from wanting a taste of her own. Flash dipped the finger again and reloaded. The moisture from Zenobia's tongue made a few more grains attach. She took his finger in her hand and slowly inserted it into her mouth.

"You doing too much lil girl!" Zenobia checked when she sucked his finger.

"My bad!" she giggled and let him go. Seconds later the warm glow of heroin swept through them all. Not quite enough for a dope fiend lean but they retreated to the sofa to bask in the euphoria.

"Five minutes!" someone shouted through the door as they knocked.

"Wow!" Zenobia reeled upon the realization that over an hour had passed.

"You good?" Flash asked as they all stood.

"Finna be!" she said and inhaled a few more lines from the table.

"Do that shit shawty!" Lacrecia cheered. They all headed out where Z-money met P-money and C-money backstage. They then separated so they could make their unique entrances. Zenobia would descend from the ceiling while P-money flew in like Supergirl. Callie opted to just walk out and rip the mic.

It would be quite the show but Flash and Lacrecia wouldn't catch it all. They rushed back to the dressing and met on the sofa. Lacrecia didn't give head when they first started creeping but now she couldn't get enough of it. As soon as they reached the coach she reached for the dick. It was enough dick to grip with one hand, stroke with the other and still had plenty to suck on.

"Damn girl!" Flash exclaimed at the spectacular blow job in process. It was so spectacular in fact that it had to be preserved for prosperity. He whipped out his phone and filmed the action. He held the phone with one hand and played in her pussy with the other. It was soon gushing in between his fingers.

As good as that mouth felt he had to pull out so he could push into that hot, little box of hers. Especially since she always let him hit raw where Zenobia always made him strap up. Two abortions was two too many so she stayed diligent. Even when he rolled over into some pussy in the middle of the night she made him wear a rubber. Lacrecia didn't though and climbed on top of his lap so he could ease inside.

"Good ass pussy!" Flash growled as he squeezed inside. He rocked and wiggled her hips until he could get a good stroke going. It wasn't long until she was bouncing up and down on the dick making squishing sounds fill the air.

"Good ass dick!" she growled herself when an orgasm began to tingle. A few more thrust and she bust a nut all over his dick. A few strokes later he did the same and filled her box to the rim like kids let out for recess.

"I gotta start pulling out," he said as he often said after busting a nut in the girl.

"Mmhm," she hummed happily and squeezed and rocked to milk him dry. She was looking for a good time to share her news and this was as good as any. "Too late now."

"Yeah, cuz I already bust," he laughed and patted her ass

so she would get up. They needed to wash up and take position side stage and support Zenobia.

"Naw, cuz I'm already pregnant," she informed.

"NICE SHOW!" Zenobia declared and clapped as the Pretty Thugs finally exited the stage after the extended show.

Being the headliner meant giving the fans what they paid their money for. That meant songs from the new album as well as favorites from the first album. They also performed their songs with the other acts on the label. Callie always showed her ass with a freestyle to close it out.

"Thanks lil mama!" she squealed and wrapped her up. She was still winded from leaving it all on stage. They were still hugged up when she noticed the look on Flash's face. He looked like his girlfriend's friend who he fucked on the side had just told him she was pregnant by him.

"Huh? Who?" Flash asked since he was baffled by the news. Only because he was a little slow. The way he had been smashing Lacrecia this should not have been a shock.

"Awe hell! He got what my baby got!" Callie laughed since Ervin had been answering questions like that lately.

"Ion know what that means," Ervin laughed and pulled her along. "Let's go!"

"Ooh, somebody tryna fuck someone!" she giggled and she was right. They skipped the dressing room and headed straight back to the hotel.

"Un-uh!" Zenobia huffed as Penny traipsed past without

a word. She rushed to her dressing room to shower, change and hit her next appearance.

"She has been acting stank lately," Lacrecia declared since that's what Zenobia wanted to hear. She agreed with her and pointed out all the ways on the way back to the hotel.

"Well, you might wanna hit the club or catch a movie," Zenobia suggested when they reached the suite. "Cuz I'm finna fuck my man..."

"He already been fucked," she snickered under her breath and headed back out. Baby or no baby she was going to get her party on. She definitely didn't intend to sit there and listen her friend fuck their man.

CHAPTER 15

"Fucking, fuck, fuck!" Callie groaned when morning made her wake up. She didn't particularly dislike morning, but hated that Ervin had to fly back to Atlanta on this particular morning.

"Yeah I know so we need to fuck, fucking fuck!" he laughed. Parting was indeed such sweet sorrow but a piece of pussy sure would help.

"Oh OK!" she sighed and lifted her leg to allow him to slide in from the side like he was stealing second base. It was more like a home run though once he got his stroke going. Her mind went to the birth control pills in her bag. His moans and groans was the perfect reminder since she knew what that meant.

"Fucking fuck!" he groaned and seized like hit with an electric current.

"That's right papi!" she cooed, squeezed and wiggled until he couldn't take it. He tapped out by pulling out and gathering her up like a comfort blanket. "Fuck it, I'm going with you!"

"I wish!" he laughed and kissed her head. It took all Ervin had to get out of the bed to hit the shower. That gave her the strength to get up and follow him under the steamy water.

They helped each wash in silence while thinking about tomorrow. Both the literal one and the ones to come. It sucked that they would wake up in different cities the next day but both were sure one of those tomorrows would last forever.

"We should get married," Ervin announced as he suds her plump breast. It was already good and clean but they are just fun to wash.

"Yeah, prolly should," Callie agreed and washed his clean dick some more. That's what the old folks mean but 'what's understood doesn't need to be explained', because they were officially engaged. The ring and plans would come later.

Callie and Ervin headed down to the lobby where the car waited to take him to the airport. Another car waited to take the group to the local radio station, photo shoots and other appearances. They may have moped but Zenobia and Flash came out laughing.

"Hey y'all!" Zenobia sang happily since she just got dicked down real good. Lacrecia moped behind them since she didn't.

"My man Erv!" Flash cheered and lifted his hand for dap. Ervin frowned at it at first, but didn't want to explain to Callie why she left him hanging.

"Yeah, sup," he said rather dryly.

"Shoot, y'all may as well ride together since y'all on the same flight!" Zenobia suggested. She was excited about their men becoming friends so they could be one big, happy family.

"Yeah cuz..." Callie started and finished by nodding her head towards Jovita and the rest of the gang coming.

"Yeah," Ervin agreed just to be agreeable. A bad habit life would one day break him of. Sometimes in life you just have to say fuck them folks and do you. The men got last hugs and kisses before their women departed.

"Hell of a show last night!" Flash bragged. He only caught half of it but that part was good too.

"Word, especially that intro!" Ervin dared since he saw when he and Lacrecia arrived well after the show began. "Your girl flew in like Wonder woman!"

"Oh yeah, dope!" he agreed, which confirmed his lie. Ervin just turned his head and tuned out whatever he was saying in favor of the city passing by the window.

"We got beautiful, talented, loving women..." he cut in on Flash talking about the game.

"Facts!" he agreed and raised his hand for another dap. This time Ervin did leave him hanging.

"Then how are you fucking their friend?" Ervin needed to know. Flash paused for a few moments to decide if he should lie or not. Lying came naturally yet seemed futile at the moment since the dude knew what was going on.

"How? Mainly face to face. Her young ass got some good ass pussy!" he laughed. Ervin didn't laugh which prompted the question, "So, you gonna snitch on me?"

"Naw, I'ma mind my business. I just wanted you to know I know so you know why I don't fuck with you," he explained plainly.

"Bet I don't buy nare another car from y'all," Flash

shrugged and turned his head too. They rode to the airport and flew back to Atlanta in first class without another word.

"SUP with the long face lil girl?" Zenobia asked when she saw Lacrecia moping as the jet descended into Dallas.

"I um..." Lacrecia was trying to think of a story other than missing her man but R Kelly began to chime on her phone. Even Zenobia knew who belonged to that ringtone.

"Tell mama I'm taking good care of you," she said and moved to give her some space to talk to her mother. Lacrecia's dad had written her off after catching her bouncing up and down on some dude's dick in his driveway. Mama bounced on a few dicks back in her day so she understood.

"Hey mama," Lacrecia greeted and got caught up on the family and hometown.

"Hey," Penny smiled when Zenobia plopped next to her since Callie was on her phone as well.

"Hey yourself," she said and looked down at her screen. "Dang girl! Eight million followers!"

"Hell yeah, they fucks with the P!" she shot back. The fans were definitely feeling P-money, but so was she. P-money was her own biggest fan.

"I see," she agreed and checked her own page. The Pretty Thugs page had over five million while her own page was just over a million. The last post was two weeks ago. "I see Death Trap posting about you!"

"Yeah, after I put that P-money on him," she snickered. That was partly why he was sprung but she was too.

"Err body all boo'd up! We need find lil girl a man,"

Zenobia said loud enough for her to hear, but didn't see the eye roll to follow. "I'ma find her a nice lil fella,"

'I got a fella and ain't shit about him lil!' Lacrecia fussed in her mind and rolled her eyes again. A sinister smile spread on her face when she thought of a sinister plan. There was no need for her to travel all over the country. She wasn't performing or doing photo shoots. She could go back to Atlanta and have Flash all to herself for the next few months.

"Girl, what's wrong with you?" Callie laughed when she saw the mischievous grin on Lecrecia's face.

"Huh?" she asked to shake it off, and get into character. Her brows furrowed and mouth pouted woefully.

"You good? Your mama OK?" Zenobia asked full of concern.

"No, she not feeling well and no one is there to help her," she moaned and threatened to cry. Some people have the uncanny ability to believe their own bullshit and Lacrecia was some people. She literally had to be consoled over some shit she just made up.

"Girl you need to go to her!" Callie insisted.

"Word!" Zenobia agreed as Penny immediately booked a flight.

"But, y'all need me too! This is my job!" Lacrecia moaned.

"No, you are our family!" Penny corrected and pulled a stack of miscellaneous hundreds from her purse. One half hour appearance would fill it right back up.

"Facts!" Zenobia and Callie agreed and broke bread as well. Lecrecia's purse was stuff with cash by the time they landed. She rushed over to the commercial terminal and headed back to Atlanta to get stuffed with dick.

THE DALLAS SHOW was nothing short of epic. The girls were back to their old selves and had a ball on stage. Callie and Penny closed out with solo songs from their new upcoming solo projects while Zenobia twerked and showed out. Houston was just as hyped and the crew grew close like they once were. San Antonio, Irvin and up to Oklahoma city were off the chain. Then, came Iowa, Montana and Idaho, Aka P-money country. That's when everything began to unravel once again.

"See what my baby is doing..." Zenobia sang as she called Flash's phone. They didn't speak last night after the show so she called the next morning.

She didn't get an answer there so she tried his business line. It too went to voicemail. She was still in the mood to talk so she called Lacrecia next. The girl hadn't called in a couple of days which was odd.

"Hmp?" she wondered when that call was deliberately sent to voicemail. Lacrecia had a mouthful of Flash at the moment so she couldn't talk.

"Sup," Callie greeted, then matched her frown. "What's wrong?"

"Ion know?" she had to ask since she wasn't exactly sure herself. Something was definitely wrong, she just couldn't put her finger on it. "You ever, y'all be, I mean. Do Ervin answer when you call? I mean, you ever can't reach him?"

"Naw, he calls me more than I can him. But you gotta know that men who be about business be busy. I don't expect him to be on call twenty four, seven," she rambled since she knew where this was going. She saw Flash's eyes flash on her breast, legs, other chicks, anytime he was around.

"You right!" she quickly accepted because she wanted to. "Now, Ion know what's up with this lil girl phone?"

"She is still with her moms. Excuse me, her mama 'ndem," Callie snickered.

"Ha ha," Penny laughed and tried Lacrecia's phone again.

'I don't see nothing wrong...' the R Kelly ringtone began to play.

"Mm-a-mm mm-m" Lacrecia hummed along with it because had far too much dick in her mouth to sing it.

"Mmhm," Flash agreed as he guided her head up and down. He switched to two hands when his legs began to twitch and tingle. She wasn't getting away this time. "Argh!"

"Un-uh! Mm-mm!" she declared and declined when the salty explosion exploded in her mouth. She was trapped in place and just had to take it until he was spent. As soon as he loosed his grip she tore off to the bathroom.

"So dramatic," Flash laughed when she came back pouting. Her whole face was wet from washing her mouth out.

"That was mean!" she pouted some more and poked her lip out. She cuddled up next to him on his sofa and rested her head. "Ion mind tho. If it makes you happy."

"It does," Flash quickly replied. That was one of the things he appreciated about the young chick. She was pliable like a lump of warm clay.

Having her and Zenobia was really having his cake and eating it too. Now he just had to figure out how to get her to the abortion clinic. She may have been naive and nice but she was also smart enough to know this baby was a meal ticket for life. Which is why she shut him down anytime he brought it up. That's why he laid plan B out on the table.

"Yay!" Lacrecia cheered at the pile of cocaine he dumped out.

"That's you. I got a thing tonight with my agent," he explained. What he didn't explain was keeping her filled with enough drugs to lose that baby.

"Want me to cook while you're out?" she asked before leaning in for a line.

"At the condo. I'll fall by later," he replied, which was his way of saying she couldn't stay in his house.

"Bring more of this!" she said and snorted a few more lines.

"Most definitely!" he laughed since that was a part of his plan.

CHAPTER 16

"Fucking Iowa," Callie chided and shook her head as she looked down at all the fields and farms.

"The only corn rows I ever seen was on a nigga head?" Zenobia frowned. What neither said was they still felt some kind of way about P-money wanting more money than them for these states. After all, she was still part of a group. Penny lifted her chin in indignation but remained silent since she knew the answer.

"Well, we have two shows booked in Boise. And..." Jovita explained then muted herself for the moment. There were things to discuss but they wouldn't be discussed as the jet touched down on the runway.

"The fuck is all that?" Callie exclaimed at the throngs of people near the hangar.

"The president prolly coming?" Zenobia guessed.

"Hmp!" P-money huffed since she knew. They would know soon too since they were headed that way. Soon they were close enough to make out the words on the signs. They were the same ones the crowd was screaming.

"The fuck!" Dominique reeled when the thunderous cheers penetrated the cabin.

'P-money! P-money! P-money!' they shouted, clapped and waved their P-money signs while wearing their P-money shirts, glasses, purses and shoes.

"Excuse me ladies. The P-hive beckons..." Penny said rather smugly as the door opened. They were hyped for the plane but they lost their minds when she stepped.

"More like children of the corn! Country ass shit!" Callie lamented but laughed.

"This bitch is one of the Beatles!" Jovita declared when a couple of girls literally passed out. Little girls were dressed in P-money outfits with P-money hairdos.

"I ain't finna wait on this bull shit," Callie fussed. She was even madder at hearing herself use the word finna.

"Word B," Zenobia used her borrowed slang. They both took off towards the terminal on foot. Jovita sighed and took off after them. Dominique stayed back with Penny.

"Hey girl! You pretty! Is that P-money lip gloss got your lips all shiny..." P-money sang as she worked the crowd.

"Hold up ladies," Jovita called as she caught up. She couldn't let these millionaire rap stars walk through the airport alone. All the security she hired stayed back to control the crowd.

"This some bull shit yo!" Callie snapped from a rush of jealousy coursing through her body. She certainly didn't feel like this when they went crazy over her in Birmingham Alabama. Nor did Z-money when her hometown showed out for her. Atlanta Georgia loved their Z-money. Her relationship with Flash made them the latest power couple in the city.

"This is part of the business ladies. Each of you have your strengths and strongholds, this is hers. Stay focussed and kill this show tonight," the boss announced like a boss.

"You mean tonight, tomorrow night and the next night," Zenobia whined since they had three nights in the city.

"Yup, and add more zeros to your bank accounts," Jovita reminded since that's what mattered most.

"I just can't wait to do my solo joint!" Callie said and was done with it.

"Me too!" Zenobia shot back. The demand for her was nowhere near that of her bandmates. She may not command the same advances and bonuses but many labels would jump at the chance to sign her. She was part of the hottest girl rap group in the world.

The Pretty Thugs slayed the show that night. Callie and Zenobia went back to the hotel while P-money did solo events and appearances. They all had to show up at the local radio show the next day. Once again they were met by a mob.

"The P-hive showed up for a bih!" P-money barked when they arrived at the station to find another big crowd with big signs. There were even a few tents lining the sidewalk since some fans spent the night. P-money went live with them throughout the night.

What everyone else in the limo noticed was Penny was P-money before she needed to be P-money. She was usually Penny until it was time to transform. That time came when the limo came to a stop and security cleared a path into the station.

"P! P-money! I love you!" the crowd screamed, fanned, fawned and fainted.

"Hey guys! Brock is waiting on you guys!" a bubbly assistant cheered and ushered them inside. Brock was a middle aged Howard Stern wannabe. He had the big hair, big voice and big mouth. A big mouth and the Pretty Thugs was always a problem.

"This isn't good," Dominique moaned. She knew these girls well enough to understand the perturbed looks on two thirds of the group's faces. She also knew both Callie and Zenobia would act on those looks.

"No, it'll be fine. Great even," Jovita offered and twisted her lips like she didn't believe it herself.

"OK Iowa! I have a special treat for you!" Brock cheered as the girls entered. The smile on his face was infectious and quickly spread around the room. "I give you, P-money and the Pretty Thugs!"

"Un-uh, nope. That's what we not doing!" Zenobia fussed.

"Nah B, it's just the Pretty Thugs. We not no Pips son," Callie barked. Dominique just shook her head hearing Callie was on her Harlem shit. That usually ended up in violence.

"It's gonna be great," Jovita pouted and shook her head.

"Oh, OK. The Pretty Thugs!" he corrected, then went left once again. "So P-money, when did you start rapping?"

"In my mama belly! I was born spitting bars..." she said. The next few questions went to P-money as well.

"Man, I ain't finna sit here..." Zenobia finally decided and stood.

"Yeah fuck this," Callie agreed and followed her out.

Brock nor Penny seemed to notice or mind their departure and continued on with the interview.

"Ladies..." Jovita called after them but Dominique shut her down.

"Let them go. It's the lesser of two evils," she reminded. The last thing they needed was another viral video of Pretty Thugs gone wild.

"HELLO?" Lacrecia answered with so much attitude it took Zenobia by surprise.

"Lacrecia?" she asked and looked at the name on her screen to make sure she didn't call the wrong number. A gentle rub on her booty took some of the snap out of her tone.

"Dis me. What's up?" she said a little better than before.

"Just checking on you girl. How's your mama?"

"My mama?" Lacrecia asked and strained her face at the question.

"Uh, yeah. You said you had to go check on her," Zenobia reminded and strained her face as well.

"Oh, she good. I'm back in the city now," she said and kissed Flash's chest. It was very important to do that while on the phone with her.

"Oh? OK, so you can just meet us in New York. This Midwest shit ain't talmbout a bitch ass thang!" Zenobia fussed. She was prepared to vent to her about P-money and her P-hive but Lacrecia wasn't in the mood.

"New York? When?" she asked as if she were doing

Zenobia a favor. She gripped Flash by the dick and gave it a lick.

"We got one more show here then we headed to New York city," she replied but didn't get a reply in return. "Hello?"

"Mmhm," she hummed with Flash snuggly in her mouth.

"Yeah, a'ight. Let me call my man. I'll holla girl," she said and got another, 'mmhm' in return.

"Hole up," Flash directed when Zenobia's pretty, pink vagina popped on his screen as it buzzed.

'Gawk' she replied and just took him deeper in her throat.

"Hey baby!" Flash cheered happily. Perhaps a little too happily since Lacrecia 'accidentally' scraped his dick with her teeth.

"Hello?" Zenobia asked since she heard the same background music she heard when she was speaking to Lacrecia a minute ago. Not that she would have guessed her head was bobbing below but the song changed before it registered fully.

"I miss you! I love you!" he cooed and got another gawk from below. Lacrecia threw her wrist and head into overdrive to disrupt the call as much as she could. Fucking the same man made her believe they were on equal footing even though Zenobia was fitting all of the bills.

"Awe baby!" she blushed and pouted and contemplated leaving right then. "I love you too! Tell me to come home and I'll say fuck these folks and come!"

"Naw, don't sssss, fuck up your money shawty," he barely managed.

"Yeah, you're right," she agreed. She still felt slighted by the offers Callie and Penny got over her. Now she needed to prove she was just as worthy. Bad news or tragedy has caused many a drug problem. Just like pride and self determination had cured just as many. Zenobia had been sober since Lacrecia left and liked it.

"You're going to New York next right? I should fly up and meet you," he offered.

"Yeah, that would be..."

"Hold on!" Flash suddenly shouted and muted his phone.

"Mmhm!" Lacrecia moaned as volcano Mount Flash erupted in her mouth. He gripped her head with two hands and made her take it all. Not that he had too since she loved to please him. It took him a couple of minutes of shivers and shakes before he could take the call again.

"Hello?" he asked, trying to sound calm but a good nut takes a lot out of a man.

"You OK? You sound..." she was saying but he sounded how he sounded when he came and she wasn't dealing with that prospect.

"Just tired. It's good to hear from you baby. Love you," he blurted. She wanted to return the sentiment but he was gone.

"Hmp?" she huffed and twisted her lips in confusion. That was such an odd call but her mind wouldn't go where her man and friend went. She just didn't think like that. Which is why wicked people are always able to take advantage of good people. Good minds aren't always able to process their wicked schemes. Still, "How did he know we were going to New York next?"

CHAPTER 17

"Mmhm," Callie snarled when the stewardess directed the passengers to fasten their seatbelts for the descent. The descent into New York's LaGuardia airport and she was already feeling cocky.

"Here we go," Dominique laughed since she knew what was coming. P-money's P-hive showed up and showed out, out west but they were now in New York city. Aka, C-money-ville.

"Oh lawd!" Zenobia laughed but Penny didn't pay her any attention. She felt some kind of way about the way they treated her on the last stops. Like they hated on her shine.

Besides, she was too busy stalking her so-called boyfriend all over the globe. His world tour put him in direct contact with some of the baddest chicks on the planet. They spoke every day but the time difference left his nights free. Free to fuck, and fuck he did. Some of the baddest chicks on the planet.

"We're booked at the Waldorf," Jovita announced as they taxied to the hangar where a limo awaited.

"Where else is there to stay in the city," Penny quipped and flipped her hair. Then pulled her shades on since she was a star and all.

"Actually, my man booked us at the Plaza. I'll see y'all tomorrow at the parade," Callie informed.

"What parade?" Zenobia asked since she missed most of what most people said to her lately. She was too confused by her man's and friend's recent behavior to grasp much of anything else.

"C-money day in Harlem," Penny chuckled like it was a joke. Actually it was kinda a big deal since all the New York celebrities would be in attendance.

"Yeah, in the world famous Polo Grounds. It's not Iowa but there's a basketball tournament, dance contest..." Callie corrected as she walked away. Ervin was waiting with a rental and she was ready to go ride him cowgirl.

"These hoes..." Zenobia said and shook her head. They had a night off so she called Flash to see if he would come knock the dew from her lily like the rising sun, but he didn't answer. She tried the next option but Lacrecia didn't answer either. She moped the rest of the ride to the hotel. She wouldn't be the only thug moping tonight.

"WELL HELLO MISS MANNING! Welcome back to the Waldorf Astoria!" the manager personally greeted when the driver opened the limo door.

"Sup yo," she greeted casually and guarded her P-money

as she stepped out. Paparazzi loved catching celebrity crotch shots as women stepped out of cars. Which is why she occasionally let one slip when she wore her P-money panties. The free publicity that followed just drove up more sales.

Zenobia incidentally gave up a nice shot of plump yellow panties as she stepped out behind her. She was still checking her boyfriend's social media pages. He was plenty active yet her calls just didn't seem to get answered. Her head tilted curiously at some of the same tags and pin drops Lacrecia had posted. They both ate at the same restaurant last night but neither of them mentioned it to her.

"Get yo head in the game shawty!" Dominique warned as they walked inside the hotel.

"Huh?" she asked in confusion and looked up and saw people looking at her. She shook it off and transformed into Z-money mode for the fans.

"Where's C-money?" a few people asked. Penny was too busy looking at Death Trap and some dusty Norwegian girl.

"Who gives a fuck!" she pouted and stomped off to her suite.

"C-money is with family. She'll see you guys uptown tomorrow at the parade and block party!" Jovita replied and rushed her frazzled clients away from the limelight.

"They may need a break?" Dominique suggested. They saw this same burnout on the first tour.

"This is the biggest show of the tour. Two shows at Madison Square Garden!" Jovita replied. Both noticed she didn't actually answer the question. Not that it mattered since they both knew the answer.

Zenobia and Penny were having man troubles but the only trouble Callie was having at the moment was trying to look behind and see her man while she rode him backwards. She was a cowgirl after all.

"THIS IS SOME BULLSHIT!" Penny protested as they rode along the C-money parade route.

"She ain't say that when those damn children of the corn were passing out in them damn corn fields!" Zenobia snapped even though she wasn't mad at her.

"Uh, yes y'all did!" Penny reminded. Just because she didn't bite on them didn't mean she didn't hear the snide remarks.

"Ladies..." Jovita said in an invitation to act ladylike. Both rolled their eyes and kept on scrolling.

"Agh!" Penny gasped when she finally found what she was looking for. The same Norwegian chick was still on Death Trap's arm but now they were in Italy.

An easy hundred thousand people tagged her in the photos to alert her to his infidelity. She couldn't ignore it even if she wanted to. Her face balled in a mix of anger and pain for the rest of the ride up to the Polo Grounds.

"What's up Harlem! Y'all remember me?" Callie gushed from the middle of the basketball court.

"Hell yeah! C-money! Lennox ave!" Harlem shouted back. She hit them with a new verse from her upcoming solo album that just pissed her bandmates off even more.

"She may as well do the fucking show by her fucking self!" Penny fumed. She was so mad she couldn't even curse straight. "Damn, fuck, shit, fuck!"

"For real! I should just go back to Atlanta," Zenobia

pondered since no one would answer their phones down there. This situation was nagging at her like a constant ringing in her ear.

"Listen, I need you ladies to keep it together. Tomorrow we perform at the Garden!" Dominique reminded. Both pouted but kept their collective cool while Callie basked in the hometown love.

"This is dope," Ervin managed to slip in while Callie greeted her adoring fans. There were people from many of the many grade schools she attended growing up. As well as now grownups from a few foster homes she once lived in. She gave autographs and took pictures with each and everyone of them.

"Hole up..." Callie snarled when she saw a familiar face not attached to a good memory. She started to get up and chase the face but it was headed right towards her.

"Sup Callie?" Demetria asked and lifted her dingy chin to make sure she could recognize her.

"Sup is you beat me out of eight grand," she growled and began to stand. Ervin was so confused he wasn't able to stop her from climbing down and jumping down the woman's face. Luckily, Callie was able to stop herself. "I ain't even trippin."

"I'm fucked up ma. Fucked around and hit that pipe one good time. That shit done held me hostage 'err since," she admitted like most won't.

"So, I know you are not asking me for no money to get high!" Callie barked and was ready to jump down her face once more.

"Nah B, I need help. I need rehab," she pouted and dropped a tear. "Them shits mad expensive though!"

"I got you," Callie heard herself say. It had to have come from her heart since it bypassed her brain. It was out now so she would stand by it.

"HEY BABY! Show finna start. I guess you are on your way up here. I left your name at the gate so you can just come on backstage. OK baby, I'm finna go tear this shit up!" Zenobia left on Flash's voicemail since he was too deep in Lacrecia to take the call. Her next call went to Lecrecia's voicemail, "Where you at lil girl? Thought you was supposed to meet me in New York?"

"Show time!" a stagehand announced as he tapped on the dressing room door. All three Thugs had their own dressing room these days so he made his rounds.

"Yeah! The fuck!" Penny protested the knock.

"Showtime!" he repeated and moved along.

"It damn sure is!" Penny decided and went live. "Yoooo dis yo bih P to the muhfuckin money! Err body tagging me in that fuck boy post. Let me tell y'all the real. Death Trap is a buster. Ion care who he fuck with cuz Ion fuck wit him! That was a publicity stunt for clout. Picture me fucking with a dude who get knocked out in public..."

"Penny...." Jovita shouted as she ran towards her dressing room. She practically tackled the girl to get the phone away from her.

"What are you doing!" Penny fussed as Jovita canceled her live.

"Girl you know that guy is unstable!" she warned. Death Trap was the most vicious troll on the internet. He was like

Fifty cent, Eminem and Tekashi all rolled into one foul mouthed person.

"Fuck he gone do to me!" she snapped and rushed the stage. Little did she know those were famous last words of many before much destruction.

C-money was still riding high off the hometown love and put on her best performance ever. Likewise, her co-thugs used their anger to fuel a vicious performance. They looked like the best of friends once again as they prowled the stage like a pack of hungry lionesses. P-money even walked on the crowd as she spit her verse. Except she switched it up and free styled a nasty dis of Death Trap. Jovita just shook her head but had to admit that shit was dope. It would be viral before they even left the stage.

"They're back!" Dominique cheered as the group literally went crazy.

"Hmp," Jovita huffed. She wasn't sure if this was a new start, or a good end.

"YOOOO! THAT SHIT WAS FUCKING LIT!" Callie cheered as they rushed from the stage.

"You kilt that cheating ass nigga!" Zenobia cheered and high-fived Penny.

"Fuck him!" she huffed and rolled her eyes. She was done with him from here on out.

The limo headed to the hottest club in the city. They could afford to pay the girls ten racks apiece to do one song. They chopped it like old times as they headed over. Zenobia rolled her eyes when she saw Flash's dick flash on her screen. She still answered tho.

"Hello?" she asked, full of attitude. She hoped he was in New York so she could pout and be mad until they had some makeup sex. She was thinking back shots were in order.

"My bad baby. Shit came up and..." he said and went into a symphony of excuses.

"Mmhm," Zenobia hummed and rolled her eyes as she accepted each and every one of them.

"The fuck sis at tho?" Penny wondered and dialed Lecrecia's phone.

"You know you gonna have to make it up to me..." Zenobia was saying. She was still thinking back shots but the familiar tune stopped her in her tracks. Her eyes blinked as she processed the R Kelly ringtone. Flash was still talking but she didn't hear a word of it.

Lacrecia sent Penny's call to voicemail but not before Zenobia heard her phone. She connected one dot that led to another dot until she had a full picture. Now, everything made sense to her. Her man and best friend had been fucking for months, right under her nose.

"What are you doing!" Callie shrieked when Zenobia snatched the door open. Luckily the limo was stopping for a light because she jumped out. It was still moving so she lost her footing.

"What the hell..." Jovita screamed as Zenobia rolled on the street before hopping up and hailing a cab. "Someone go after her!"

"Go after her where?" Callie shot back. "Where is she going!"

"I know where she is going..." Penny said and hopped out

of the car as well. Several yellow cabs crossed lanes and skidded to a stop to pick up the white woman. "Take me to the airport!"

"Uh, which one?" the driver asked.

"Um...." Penny hummed since she didn't know.

"LaGuardia!" he decided for her since that was the white people's airport. He didn't bother with the meter since he was going to charge her white people prices. She paid it without batting an eye and got out.

Penny rushed through the airport bumping into people from looking up at the departure boards. The next flight to Atlanta would be boarding soon so she took off towards the ticket counter.

"Hey! Yo! Fuck outa here!" people shouted as she cut the line. Word spread about who she was and the disgruntled became gruntled.

"Atlanta!" she shouted and pointed at the flight number.

"That flight is boarding now. The next one..." the woman was saying but P-money popped her head out and took over.

"Ain't no next one! Dis a damn emergency!" she shouted. A white woman shouting in LaGuardia was sure to get attention and the manager came rushing over.

"Is everything OK?" he asked the white woman instead of his employee.

"I need to be on that flight!" she fussed.

"That's the second one!" he said and nodded at the clerk, who swiped the card. He had just escorted someone to that same gate through the employee sections. It would be close but they took off in hopes of catching the plane before it taxied out to the runway. They jumped on a luggage carrier and made it just in the nic of time.

Zenobia was rocking back and forth in her seat like she was off her meds. She was already mad enough until someone plopped down beside her in the half filled plane. She lifted her head to snap but got snapped on instead.

"Girl, are you crazy jumping out of moving vehicles! In Man-damn-hattan of all damn places!" Penny fussed.

"Man," Zenobia pouted, then lost it. It took a good while to get the story out through the tears and sobs. By the time the plane landed in Atlanta Penny was just as mad as she was.

CHAPTER 18

"Shit!" Flash grunted as that tingly feeling spread throughout his body. It started in his toes, shot up to his brain, then exploded from the tip of his dick. If there was one good thing about her pregnancy was not having to worry about getting her pregnant.

Flash was pretty reckless in general but always worried after the fact. Now he could bust in her until his heart's content. Plus she was a lot more pliable than his woman. No nagging, no demanding. In fact, Lacrecia was more like a living sex doll than a woman.

"Come on, give it up!" she pleaded. Then squeezed her tight little box and took it.

"Fuck!" he grunted this time and filled her up once again for the day. She was better stocked than most sperm banks at the moment.

"Mmhm," she cooed and rubbed his back as he searched for his breath. They both could have gone to sleep right then but didn't. He pulled out, popped up and hit the living room.

"Got us some new shit," Flash announced as they traipsed naked to the front room where his pants were.

"Yay!" she cheered even though she knew it was time to stop using. Pliable or not, she knew this baby in her belly was a meal ticket for life.

"Let's see what this thang talking about..." he said and dumped some of the powder out on the coffee table. He chopped, crushed, sorted and made lines. A rolled up hundred dollar bill made perfect straws even if Lacrecia always swiped them while they got high. Flash inhaled the thicker, longer lines he made for himself and passed her the hundred.

"Dang!" Lacrecia laughed when Flash immediately fell back on the sofa. His eyes rolled in his head as he laid on his back. She had been on the fence about using it but if it was that good she had to have some. She leaned in and inhaled one line and realized something was wrong. She didn't even get to steal the bill before she fell out beside him.

"WHERE TO?" Penny asked as they stomped through Atlanta's Hartsfield Jackson airport.

"Buckhead! They at his house!" Zenobia declared.

"Pretty Thugs! P-money! Z-money!" fans called as they marched militarily towards a waiting Uber.

"Hey! I just saw that video!" the driver cheered when he recognized the celebrities in his car.

"Can you just take us to the address, Please!" Penny popped off. She had been in a bunch of videos and had no idea what he was talking about.

"I got you," he said and made sure his rearview mirror cam was on. At least he had proof of this famous fare for posterity.

"Just wait on us. I got a nice tip for you," Penny said when they reached Flash's mini mansion.

"Hmp!" Zenobia huffed when she didn't see Flash's Rolls in the driveway. The Lamborghini truck was present which meant he could be too.

She had the element of surprise when she entered the code into the door to gain entry. Penny was right on her heels when she rushed into the living room. They were going to jump Flash's big ass, but the room was empty. They heard a TV playing and took off up the stairs and into his bedroom.

"Yeah nigga!" Zenobia yelled as she kicked the door open. The bed was empty so she rushed into the bathroom, "Un-huh! Oh."

"See, she wouldn't do that. He might, but lil girl? Nah, we been too good to her," Penny sighed.

"Unless..." Zenobia began and nearly cried at the thought.

"No way. Nah, man," Penny said and shook the thought from her head. "Let's just go back to New York. I just lost ten racks fucking with you."

"OK, you're right. I know they ain't at my crib," she agreed. "And you talmbout some, ten racks! Girl you make that in a 'coupla minutes!"

"Still," Penny laughed as they headed back out to the Uber. The driver was so distracted he didn't notice them approaching until they pulled the door open. "Ewww!"

"My bad! I was just!" he said and tried to put his dick away but it was too hard from pulling on it to the video on his phone. He just covered the erection and turned off his screen.

"Mmhm," Penny laughed. "Take us back to the airport."

"I just gotta swing by the condo. Grab my thing, I forgot my, mmhm," Zenobia said.

"Mmhm," Penny agreed since she understood. What she was sure of was no way was lil girl in her condo with her man. "Let's grab it so we can head back to the airport. What we not 'bout to do is fuck up our bread over no dudes!"

The ride over the building was as quiet as the night before Christmas. The driver was babbling about something that neither of the passengers heard. They were too busy wondering if they would ever be happy. Perhaps there was a curse on them.

"Um, excuse me..." the driver announced after a few minutes of sitting. They both looked up and recognized they were parked in front of their building.

"Why you ain't say shit!" Zenobia fussed and popped the man in the back of his head. "Should give yo ass a bad review!"

"Don't press charges. She's sorry!" Penny gushed and fished out a hundred from her purse.

"We good," he said now that he had a hundred bucks. He looked at both of their asses as they headed inside the building. Then went back to the P-money porn he had been jacking off to before. Their first stop was the garage to make sure they didn't see Flash's car.

"Why not take my parking spot," Zenobia sighed when she saw his Rolls Royce sitting regally in her parking spot.

"That don't mean nothing!" Penny declared as they

headed inside. Zenobia sure didn't want it to mean anything so she nodded her head.

"I know, right" she laughed and pressed the elevator call button. It popped open immediately whether they were ready or not.

The ride up to Zenobia's floor was short and tense. The elevator never moved that fast before but then again she never dreaded going home this bad before. They both dragged their feet down the hallway and talked louder than necessary to be heard inside. Plenty of warning not to get caught in the act of anything.

"Man..." Zenobia moaned and opened the door. They both got stuck trying to process the naked people on her sofa. It looked like they had fucked themselves to sleep right there, on the spot. There was a delayed reaction before Zenobia got pissed and struck.

"In my house! On my ten thousand dollar sofa!" she screamed as she hopped the thousand dollar coffee table. Penny was right behind her as they pounced on Flash.

"Uh, Z..." Penny paused and pulled her friend away when she realized they were both unresponsive. She then recognized the foam coming from Flash's bluish lips. "Call 9-11!"

"Oh shit! Oh shit!" Zenobia shouted and complied. The high rent prefix of the house phone meant an operator answered immediately. She didn't wait for the woman to ask what was her emergency before telling her. "I have two dead bodies in my living room!"

❄

"LOOKS LIKE ANOTHER ONE," the paramedic declared as he entered. There had been a rash of overdoses lately so he counted these amongst them.

"Another two you mean," his partner said as he came in behind them. Each took a body so they could pronounce a time of death to correspond with their arrival.

"No, one. This one has a pulse!" he shouted and began treatment with Narcan. They had so many overdoses they knew exactly how to treat them. A second pair of paramedics arrived to help out.

"She's alive!" Penny cheered from the doorway since Zenobia had stepped outside.

"Mmhm," Zenobia hummed. A grimace spread on her face when she accepted she didn't care one way or the other. She had dealt with so much death she was numb to it. Plus, she had been fucked over enough to finally arrive at the conclusion of, fuck them folks.

She just blinked as Lacrecia was wheeled away while they still worked on her. A beat cop stayed behind to wait for the detectives. Her head tilted curiously as she ran her eyes over the long shape of Flash's dead body under a sheet.

"He's hard!" she pointed at the dick print visible through the sheet. Penny's eyes went wide at the inappropriate observation but her full bladder took priority.

"She's in shock!" one of the remaining paramedics declared and came over to help out. "Take this, it'll calm you."

"I'm calm," Zenobia declared but recognized the pill and took it anyway.

"No!" Penny shouted when she came back just as she tossed her head back to swallow the pain pill. "What did you give her!"

"Just something to take the edge off," the lady paramedic said.

"Bitch you just put the edge back on!" she declared since the difference between Zenobia on pills verses not on pills was as distinct as the day is from the night.

"What do we have here?" a detective asked as he came down the hall. He stopped in his tracks when he and Zenobia locked eyes. "Zenobia Lowe. Remember me?"

"Mmhm, detective Robbie. You the one got my brother kilt," she recalled.

"And who did you get killed tonight?" he asked but didn't wait for an answer. "Officer, escort these two to the precinct for an interview."

"ION KNOW SHIT! Don't know him, don't know her. It don't matter how many ways you ask me, the answer is the same," Penny fussed as soon as detective Robbie entered the interview room. The cops had taken her phone when they arrived and she was having serious social media withdrawals.

"I didn't even ask you anything, yet," Robbie smiled and attempted to turn on the charm.

"And you not! If I'm under arrest then where is my lawyer!" she shot back.

"No, you're not under arrest I just..." he was saying but Penny hopped up and headed for the door. He had already run her name and knew all about her. None of it would help with this case so he got up and went to try his luck with Zenobia.

"Bruh, what the fuck?" Zenobia wanted to know when

the detective walked in. A few hours ago she was on stage performing, now she was shivering in an ice cold police interview room.

"That's what I'm trying to figure out?" he asked since he was having trouble making sense of this. "OK, you're dating Flash?"

"I was. He downgraded tho," she shrugged.

"And, Lacrecia is..."

"Was my friend. Until she started fucking my man," she said with another shrug. The pill had kicked in now so she was feeling pretty good. "I need my phone."

"Few more questions?" he asked and asked them. "Where do you guys usually get your dope from?"

"Nigga, I know you know I just rocked Madison Square Garden! That's in New York city if you ain't know. I couldn't reach my man so I rushed down and found them dead," she relayed and stood since she was done too.

"Your friend Lacrecia survived!" he happily reported.

"Oh, OK," she shrugged and left the room.

CHAPTER 19

"Ugh!" Penny fussed as she waited for Zenobia to come from the interview room. She was ready for a good few hours of sleep in her own bed. Then fly back up to New York for the next show. Life wouldn't be that easy because as soon as she turned her phone on it buzzed nonstop with the influx of messages, DMs, emails and inbox messages.

"What sex tape!" she demanded when she saw the common theme. She clicked the link along with a million before her and, "Oh my God!"

There was Death Trap digging her out real, real good. She remembered the exact night when this took place. She had recorded him eating her out but he propped the phone on her night stand and gave her the business. She now understood his antics during the sex session. He was putting on for the camera.

"You like this Death Trap dick? Huh? All, in them guts!" the onscreen Death Trap proclaimed.

"If you would, just, shut up, and fuck me," the onscreen

Penny proposed. Death Trap complied and lifted her legs onto his shoulders and delivered the dick like grub hub. She came followed by him and the after sex conversation played out for the world to see and hear.

"Awe man..." she pouted when she watched herself get out of bed and walk to the bathroom.

"Twerk something for me baby!" he called after her. Penny only hit him with a quick shimmy but whoever edited the video made it loop as her music played.

"They said she lived!" Zenobia informed when she came out and saw her friend in tears.

"I'm dead though!" Penny wailed. Zenobia wasn't sure what was wrong yet so she just wrapped her up and let her cry. The scene caused stares from the people waiting around. Penny thought they were looking because they all saw the video. She hopped up and ran from the precinct with Zenobia on her heels.

"Wait! Hole up! I sent for an Uber." she called and caught up. Jovita called again so she quickly took her call. "Hello?"

"Is Penny with you?" Jovita asked in a whisper as the jet sped south to Atlanta.

"Yeah. She's right here," she said and began to pass the phone.

"No! Just stay with her. I'm on the way,"

"Yeah we're gonna be up in her spot. Mine a crime scene," Zenobia huffed and hung up. The police said she couldn't return until they cleared the unit. That meant searching her entire condo thoroughly. One crime scene tech was so thorough he sniffed the panties in the hamper for evidence.

Penny was glad to have some company since her phone was off. She was too embarrassed to deal with whatever fallout was coming from her sex tape. Her head shook at the little girls who looked up to and dressed like her. The teens and young women who wore P-money lip gloss and panties. An audible moan escaped her throat at the relief that her parents weren't alive to see this.

"I know," Zenobia agreed, yet for her own reasons. Every camel has a straw that will break its back and this was hers. Her mouth watered at the thought of a nice, thick line of coke. She would have to just romance it in her mind for now. The news about the star athlete overdosing in the rap star's condo was just breaking. Zenobia turned her phone off as well to avoid the gawkers and stalkers looking for an inside scoop.

"THE DOOR!" Zenobia called from Penny's sofa.

"Yeah, yeah," she groaned on her way to open it. A peep through the peephole confirmed it was one of the very few who knew where she lived. "Hey,"

"Hey," Jovita replied stoically and plopped onto the loveseat. She twisted her lips and searched for the words.

"I didn't consent to that! It was behind my back," Penny protested. "I'm going to have them take it down and sue anyone who..."

"Yeah," Jovita agreed when she shook her head at the fallacy. The sex tape went viral over night. It belonged to the universe now and there was no taking it back. "Still, we'll get in front of this. Record some warning videos for girls."

"What are y'all talking about?" Zenobia winced as she sat up and turned her phone on. It only took a few seconds for her to get an answer. Her eyes went wide and she rotated her phone for a better look. "Dang!"

"No, your situation is worse. I'm so sorry!" Jovita whined. "Don't worry about the arrangements, I'll..."

"Man, fuck them folks," Zenobia cut in. "You think this gonna mess us up?"

"Oddly enough, no," Jovita sighed. She had worked the phones in the wee hours of the night to get feedback. So far the girls were viewed as victims. Zenobia's being a thousand miles away made her an afterthought in the situation. The story was the star athlete joining the legions of Americans overdosing on fentanyl every day.

Penny benefited from the fact that it was obvious she didn't know she was being recorded. Not that it mattered since this was an age where celebrities showed their genitals for 'likes'. None of the companies interested in her solo project had backed out. One even increased their signing bonus.

"Where is Callie?" Penny finally asked.

"She's still in New York," Jovita reported reluctantly.

"What about the show tonight?" Zenobia moaned. Penny looked up for the answer that changed when she saw their faces. They had been through a lot so she sighed and pulled her phone to postpone the show.

"I'll cancel..." Jovita sighed again and made the call. Luckily for her, Dominique stayed behind so she could do the dirty work.

※

"THIS IS HER NOW," Dominique announced when Jovita's name popped on her screen. She had met with Callie and Ervin for brunch while awaiting word from Atlanta.

"Put her on speaker!" Callie requested since she was concerned about her friends. Ervin stood from the table to extradite himself from the conversation.

"Hey girl. Callie with me on speaker," Dominique greeted and warned since it's slick grimy not to inform someone if they are on speaker or another party on the line. Theirs was a grimy business but they tried to stay above it. As much as they could, for as long as they could because in the end, this was a grimy business.

"Z OK? The news said dude ain't make it?" Callie asked from the scant info gleamed from the news. Ervin actually heard it first from ESPN.

"Z is good. Penny is good. Been a crazy night," she replied to set the tone.

"Good!" both Callie and Dominique cheered into the phone. Callie added on with, "P gonna be good. Don't nobody care about no sex tape really. Err body doing it!"

"Not everyone!" Dominique warned motherly across the table.

"Never that!" Callie laughed. She and Ervin had just recorded themselves last night but he wasn't a hoe like Death Trap so no one would ever see it.

"So, in lieu of everything, I think it best we postpone tonight's show," Jovita reasoned.

"Hell naw!" Callie shot back instantly. "This is the Garden! Why should I fuck up my dough because them chicks can't keep they shit together!"

"I, um. I mean..." Jovita stammered. Not only was she

taken aback, she didn't have an answer. Especially with the wounded girls looking in her mouth. She tried to keep the same smile pasted on her face for them.

"She's right," Dominique cosigned after a second to think about it. At the end of the day Callie was her client and she had to protect her interest over anyone else's.

"She is? I mean, maybe but if they..." Jovita was asking but Callie already had the answer.

"If one monkey don't stop no show, Ion see how two would! This is my city! My time to shine and I'm not letting no one fuck it up!" she explained. She was sorry she wasn't sorry but still added, "I'm sorry but what about me? I ain't about to lose a six figure night cuz them chicks can't keep their shit tight!"

"We can call out a few A list performers?" Dominique asked even though she knew the answer. She even had them in mind since several had reached out for Callie to do cameos in their videos and verses on upcoming projects.

"You could, but," Jovita began and paused to find the best way to put this. If Callie did the show solo it would be the point of no return.

"Yeah, I know. The end of the Pretty Thugs," Dominique spelled out plainly for all.

"I'm here for it," Callie voted and sat back.

"I'll let them know," Jovita said and lifted her chin. She had accepted their fate.

"Let us know what?" Zenobia asked with a bit of attitude.

"The tour is over," she relayed. It would cost a few million in lost revenue but the album sales were strong. Even the first album was selling and streaming briskly.

"Good! I'm ready for my solo shit!" P-money declared.

Thanks to the sex tape the timing couldn't be better. The demand was high and someone would have to drop a big check to land her solo project.

"Me too!" Zenobia added, even if her demand was far less. Especially once C-money ripped Madison Square Garden solo.

CHAPTER 20

C allie solidified herself as a solo artist when she held down the concert all by herself. Having a few famous friends didn't hurt either since everyone from Jay-Z, Cardi B and Fat Joe joined her on stage. She had made quite a name for herself from her freestyles so she dropped a verse on some of the hottest songs in hip hop.

Jovita offered to send a jet for them to fly back to Atlanta but Dominique had already booked first class flights. She opted to fly business class herself since Callie's man was with her and three's a crowd. Some more details from Atlanta reached them on the way back to Atlanta.

"Whaaaaat!" Callie reeled when she recognized the name. "Lacrecia McCoy, that's Lil girl! So, he must have been hitting that while we were on tour!"

"Been hitting that," Ervin blurted with relief as if he had been holding his breath.

"Huh?" Callie asked but started formulating the answer

for herself. "You knew! That's why you be acting funny around him!"

"Funny my ass. Ain't no funny, I just don't like dude. He foul," Ervin explained. He was just big when it came to trust and honor.

"So, why you ain't tell me!" she whined and poked her lip out.

"Cuz, I don't want us in their business," he shot back.

"Bruh, they are my business tho!" Callie clapped.

"Not no more," he reminded and extended his hand. She was still a little pouty as she examined it before taking it.

"Make sure ain't no more secrets in there!" Callie giggled and squeezed. She didn't let go again until they landed in Atlanta.

"Are you ready for this?" Dominique asked when they got off the plane. She knew she was but still wanted to hear it.

"Hells yeah!" Callie shot back immediately. Going independent meant turning down a shit load of cash and spending money instead. They had a good offer in place from Jovita but that still let several million get by her. She would rather spend a mil up front and rake it all back in.

"Well, rest up and be ready to go on Monday. I'll talk to Jovita," Dominique said and gave her a hug.

"You wanna come with me to the hospital to see lil girl?" Callie asked Ervin but rephrased when he answered with his face. "Better yet, will you come to the hospital with me?"

"Since you put it like that," he laughed since those were two different questions. Men do things for their woman they don't necessarily want to do in general. Especially watching chick flicks but chicks have a vagina, so they do it.

"You might just get you some booty later," she laughed and proved me right.

"Definitely getting some booty," he corrected. They chopped it up all the way through the terminal and took a taxi to the hospital.

"Ooh, there go that nasty man!" Callie whispered when she saw Lecrecia's grandfather prowling the waiting room.

"The preacher?" Ervin reeled. He thought she was exaggerating until he watched him solicit several women. He couldn't hear what was being offered but it got him slapped.

"No! Absolutely not!" Mr McCoy was saying as he and his Mrs stepped from the elevator.

"But, we cain't leave her in the streets!" Mrs McCoy pleaded desperately.

"Woman, that child is for the streets and she is not stepping foot back in my house!" he said, and meant, and was done with it. Mrs McCoy and Callie locked eyes for a split second before the woman ducked her head and followed her husband.

"Aww man! She ain't gonna have n where to go!" Callie pouted and explained who they were. "I know Z not going to let her stay there after this."

"She can come stay with us," Ervin offered quickly.

"Nigga I..." Callie started to snap until she saw the smirk on his face. Her head nodded when she realized he got her back for the dress the night of the album release party.

"We'll rent her a place," he said. Her parents might leave her on the streets but they wouldn't.

"Hey?" Callie literally asked since Lacrecia looked like her old self laying in a hospital bed. Just like the scared little girl they met in the dorms instead of the hard, street chick she had become.

"Man, I really messed up this time," Lacrecia pouted. She would have bet she was all cried out after her parents visit but a fresh batch of tears streamed down her face.

Callie wanted to comfort her but what could she say? It was fucked up and she had no idea if everything would be alright. And, she didn't even know just how bad things were just yet. She was about to find out though.

"At least the baby lived," Lacrecia said and twisted her lips like she wasn't sure how to feel about that.

"What baby!" Callie shrieked. "Girl, tell me you are not pregnant by Zenobia's boyfriend!"

"I'm gonna grab a, mmhm, yeah..." Ervin stammered and got up out of there. Lacrecia could only cry since she certainly couldn't say that.

"What the hell is wrong with you? Huh! What happened to that sweet little, country girl we met?" Callie pleaded. Lacrecia inhaled and bit the inside of her cheeks like she used to do when she used to think. Thinking was something she hadn't done much of lately. Lately all she used her head for was for Flash to hold while giving him head.

"I'm pretty sure it's the music. And the drugs," she nodded. The answer was so truthful she had almost forgotten that Callie made some of that music that corrupted her. "My bad! I'm sorry!"

"Nah, don't be," Callie sighed. She wouldn't be responsible for the drugs but the music part hithome. She couldn't help but think about some of her own lyrics. Have her rhymes tell it, life was all about money, clothes and bros. Takes a special kind of person who can acknowledge being part of a problem and not do anything to fix it. Callie was special, but not that kind of special. She was going to do something to fix it.

"Are you mad at me?" Lacrecia pouted. After the harsh words her father laced her with she needed some kindness. Maybe the next visitor might have some though because Callie didn't.

"Fuck yeah! Stupid ass shit yo smart ass be doing! Touch my man and I'ma fucking..." Callie cut the death threat short when she began to whimper again. "OK, OK lil girl! No, I ain't mad at you. I got you, but you gonna have to do what I tell you to do!"

"Anything! You name it!" Lacrecia cheered but the snot bubble that popped out of her nose threw it off a little.

"That's what's up. And if it's a girl you can name her Callie after her auntie Callie," Callie sang. Once Lacrecia cleared up the snot bubble situation she leaned in and hugged her. "Don't worry about Z. I'll talk to her."

"FUCK THAT HOE ASS BITCH," Zenobia replied rather calmly. She was done being mad and wasn't going to be sad. Not for people who used her. Not for people who took advantage of her.

"Yeah," Callie nodded, then had another question. "Where is your sofa?"

"In the dump I hope. They were fucking on it I guess. That's where we found they naked assess," she explained, which explained why they were seated on large pillows on the floor.

"I guess I better tell you the rest..." Callie sighed.

"There's more?" Zenobia laughed incredulously. It was pretty bad as it was so what more could it be. It didn't take much to figure out. "Nuh-uh? The lil bitch was pregnant!"

"Huh? Oh, yeah," Callie sighed since that wasn't the news she came to hand deliver. "I blame him for that tho. He is, well, he was a grown ass man. Skeeting in that lil girl like he ain't got no sense!"

"Yeah, fuck them folks tho," Zenobia repeated and shrugged. She was so over it she didn't even throw Lecrecia's clothes off the balcony like her first mind suggested. "When we supposed to go back on tour?"

"We don't," Callie replied. She saw her opening and took it. "The tour is over. The group is over. I'm finna do my solo joint."

"You said finna. That shit is just in yo vocab now girl!" Zenobia deflected. Hearing it from her hit a lot different than when Jovita said it. Now it was real. "Dang."

"Nope! Un-uh! Ain't no dang!" Callie protested. "We was broke as fuck a year ago! Now we rich as fuck! I bug out err time I check my account. And I check that shit every damn day!"

"I don't. Not any more," Zenobia confessed. Money was still pouring in so there was no need. Anytime she went on a shopping spree the money was replenished by the next show.

"I really could walk away from all this shit today. I'm only doing cuz I got some shit to get off my chest," Callie said as her thoughts went back to Lecrecia's words. She may not have been a part of the problem but wasn't a part of any solution either and that's the same thing.

"Me too! P said they were talking like, five mil for her

solo project! I'm finna do the same thing!" Zenobia proclaimed. Now it was Callie's turn to be at a loss for words. She knew from Dominique that the offers for a Z-money solo project were nowhere near what she and Penny were getting. The offers were even fewer since the cocaine scandal. This latest fiasco threatened to wipe the rest away as well.

"Word," Callie said, because that's what New Yorkers say when there's nothing to be said.

"WHO?" Penny asked and peeped through her peephole. She wasn't really in the mood for company but she and Callie needed to talk. She pulled the door open and let her inside. "Sup."

"Sup with you? You good?" Callie asked as she looked around the swank condo.

"Done a few things since that one time you were here," Penny quipped to remind her that she hadn't been over since she first bought the place.

"You good tho?" Callie replied and sidestepped the remark. Her man was waiting downstairs so she didn't want to waste time going back and forth. Especially since Penny hadn't been to her house ever. Which of course would lead back to Callie not inviting her.

"I mean, I feel violated as fuck. I can't believe dude would do me like that," Penny pouted. Most injuries are exacerbated by the insult of betrayal. Because only those closest can truly betray a person.

"And he'll get his," Callie shot back as usual. She was a

huge proponent of the get back. The recompense, the pay back, vengeance and revenge.

"Already getting it," she laughed. Death Trap underestimated P-money's pull with the masses of people. She flicked on the massive TV to see if he was still on the news. A gamble since the top stories alternated between him, her and Flash's overdose.

Jovita's strategy of playing victim worked like a charm. Now women and teen girls from coast to coast were coming forward with allegations against the rap/rocker. Charges were filed in several states and he would be arrested the moment he landed back in the states. He got smart and bought a place in Bali since there was no extradition treaty with America.

'The surviving victim in the latest, high profile overdose is set to be released from the hospital today. It's unclear what relationship she had with the late basketball star or his famous girlfriend. Z-money of the Pretty Thugs has had her own public struggles with drugs...'

"They've been dragging Z," Callie sighed and shook her head. Actually the media likes to drag anyone who is doing anything good.

'Looks like trouble within the group' the pop news reporter reported. Her own career never took off so she got a job attacking those who did. 'Check out how P-money felt about the parade for C-money in her Harlem hometown'

"This is some bullshit" Penny said on someone's phone who caught the slight and sold it to media outlets.

"Dang, that's how you feel!" Callie reeled.

"That's how I felt! Same way you felt when my people

showed out in Iowa!" she reminded. She was right too but Callie still stood and walked towards the door.

"See you on the charts ma," she tossed over her shoulder on her way out.

"Yup, below my number one!" Penny shot back. She grabbed her phone and called Jovita immediately. "I'm ready!"

CHAPTER 21

"Good morning ladies," Jovita greeted as Dominique and Callie entered her office.

"Jovita," Dominique nodded on behalf of her and her client.

"So formal," she laughed even if she knew what was coming. Callie was smart and Dominique was savvy so it wasn't hard to tell their next move.

"We are not trying to be ungrateful," Callie offered almost apologetically. "Or disloyal..."

"Loyalty starts with yourself. You know what's on the table. Five million advance. Same recoup, same terms as your group deal. Except you're not splitting it three ways," Jovita laid out plainly.

The offer was meant by a moment of silence. Dominique muted herself since it was wholly her client's decision to make. Jovita had figuratively placed five million dollars on the desk. Once it was recouped through sales and streaming she would get sixty percent. Worth easily another few million.

On the flip side was putting up a mil or so of her own money and keeping eighty percent after distribution. That meant a difference of several million dollars. Plus the distinct honor of being her own boss and calling her own shots. That part was priceless.

"That's a generous offer. However, I just want, no, need to do my own thing," she declined.

"And I can't blame you! Of course we'll still provide all support on the two albums we have now," Jovita told her and turned to Dominique. "Are you staying, or leaving?"

"I'm with you. Ion see no conflict?" she answered and asked and looked between the two. Neither had any objections so it was settled. "We'll talk about distribution once the record is ready."

"I know it's gonna be hot!" Jovita cheered and stood since the meeting was over.

"As fuck!" Callie exclaimed. They shook hands before they departed the office. Penny had just exited the elevator. Callie felt some kind of way about the parade dis. She lifted her chin and walked right by her. "Tuh!"

"Tuh my ass," Penny huffed and clicked her Manolo Blahnik heels as loud as possible as she headed in for her meeting.

"Good morning Penny. Come on it," Jovita greeted as if she hadn't just stormed in.

"On God , if you sign her I'm going somewhere else!" she vowed.

"Well, I'll be honest with you. We just had a conversation

about signing," Jovita said, careful to tightrope on the truth. "As far as I'm concerned, you are the priority!"

"As I should be!" Penny declared. Jovita offered her the same deal she just offered to Callie. It matched or exceeded all other offers in the industry. The only difference was Jovita would actually pay her according to terms. Most labels looked for any rhyme or reason to beat their artist of what they agreed to pay them. No one knew that better than Tiffany who just gave birth to Mike's son broke and alone.

"SUP LIL MAMA," Zenobia sang as she breezed into the hospital room. Tiffany was in bed with her newborn sleeping on her chest.

"Hey Z!" the young lady cheered, happy not to be alone.

"Girl yo hair is a mess!" Zenobia teased and tilted her head to get a closer look at the child.

"Maybe cuz I just pushed a person out of my coochie!" the new mother exclaimed.

"A boy?" she guessed from the blue blanket.

"And look just like his no good daddy!" Tiffany said and twisted her lips so she wouldn't cry. She didn't have to though because the pain was evident in her eyes.

"What he 'talmbout?" Zenobia asked, making the woman's eyes grow wide.

"I ain't told him!" she shouted in a whisper and looked around to make sure he couldn't hear her. The fact that he put a hit on her embryo still had her shook up. "Girl, he came to my mama's apartment while I was at work. I ain't never go back. Been staying with my cousin err since. And she is taxing me to stay on her sofa!"

"Cuz, you a Real Pretty Thug! You rich!" Zenobia teased lightheartedly but that struck a nerve too.

"Chile, I ain't seen nare 'nother penny from that nigga!" she fussed. She had managed to dodge the other triggers but this one started the water works.

"Bih, no! That's what we not finna do! Ain't no tears over no nigga!" she insisted. It wasn't just a show of words either since Flash's funeral was yesterday and she didn't drop a drop from her eyes. She didn't even show up to the star studded affair. Instead she got some coke, weed and liquor so she could party like a rockstar.

"You right, I'm good," Tiffany said and got herself together.

"You finna be good. I got you," Zenobia decided on the spot. She could pay a year's rent, diapers, and formula with one of her monthly checks. Plus, she had a meeting with Jovita to discuss her future.

"You sure? I know y'all breaking up!" Tiffany revealed.

"Yeah, I'm good," she assured her.

"Oh OK. Ole girl been talking crazy today!" she said and shook her head.

"Who?" Zenobia asked but already headed for P-money's IG. She was just going live so she tuned in and turned it up.

'That's right, P-money going solo on that ass! Had to drop that dead weight. Tired of bitches sharing my shine! Get your own shine!'

"She must be higher than me!" Zenobia laughed. It was pretty funny since she was high now. Penny was stone sober, just mad. And went on...

'I been P-money since fucking high school! These broads bit my name! Bit my dance! The Money dance, that was me! They bit my whole style! *Now they Money dis and money dat! Fuck outa here...*'

"Y'all don't even rap the same!" *Tiffany challenged in Zenobia's defense. Which was correct since they all had distinct styles. It was what made their group's songs so appealing to the whole country. It was also why they had such promise as solo artists.*

'Five milly deal bitches! Fuck with it!' *Penny proclaimed and Zenobia heard enough.*

"Don't worry lil mama. I got you!" *she said and turned to leave. Zenobia made a call over to their old apartment building and reserved a two bedroom apartment. She would swing by the bank for a check to cover the twenty four thousand dollar tab when she finished her business. First, she had to swing by the label for a meeting with her manager/ CEO.*

"HEY THERE ZENOBIA," *Jovita* greeted when she arrived for her afternoon meeting.

"Mmhm," she hummed and took a seat across from her desk.

"I know there's been a lot going on. Personal and business," she began and left a strategic pause. Zenobia had lost a few sponsors from the first scandal. More jumped ship after this latest mishap. "We still believe in you though."

"Good cuz I'm ready to go crazy!" Zenobia cheered. She may have been the weak link lyrically but she made up for it with her hype.

"Great! We prepared a contract already. Same terms as the group deal, except of course you don't have to split it with anyone," Jovita said and pushed the prepared paperwork across the desk.

"Mmhm. OK. Yup, yup," she hummed and agreed as she read through the contract. It was pretty much the same as she signed before but she was looking for something in particular. She found it but it wasn't what she was expecting. "Um, my advance?"

"Yes. Five hundred thousand dollars. Standard recoupment from..."

"Naw, five hundred racks tho? Y'all gave Penny wack ass five million!" she shot back hotly.

"Well, she does have ten million more followers than you. The P-hive, the cosmetic line, the..." Jovita laid out.

"The sex tape!" Zenobia tossed in and crossed her arms.

"Yes, and you dear are in the midst of yet another drug scandal," Jovita reminded as well. "A superstar athlete died in your condo Zenobia! Honestly, we don't know how this will affect your sales. We are really taking a chance. A chance I'm willing to take."

"Well, I'm ain't! I wish I would sign for ten percent of what y'all gave Penny. Fuck that!" she decided and stood. Zenobia lifted her chin and marched out with her head held high.

Zenobia was still fussing and cussing when she reached her destination. She was a lot of things to a lot of people but a liar wasn't one of them to none of them. She told Tiffany she had her and she had her. There were plenty of apartments in and around Atlanta but this was the only one she knew best. She wasn't the only one.

"The fuck you doing here! Ion fuck with you!" Zenobia fussed when she saw Lacrecia in the office.

"I, I, we..." she stammered and pouted on the verge of crying once more.

"She is with me. I'm finna get her an apartment," Callie explained.

"Whatever! You need to get her shit out of my spot before I throw that shit in the trash!" she fussed and turned to walk off. "Bitches all fucking grimy!"

"How I'm grimy?" Callie demanded and caught her by the arm.

"Get yo hands off me bitch!" Zenobia snapped and snatched away. "You grimy for fucking with the enemy! After how that hoe snaked me and you fucking with her! And we can hit if you don't like anything I said!"

"Let's get to it then!" Callie agreed and threw up her hands. Zenobia was contradicting herself since she was there to rent an apartment for Tiffany, who Callie considered an enemy.

"Un-uh y'all!" Lacrecia pleaded and jumped between them before they could come to blows. Both were about to go through her until she pointed at all the phones pointed at the celebrity sighting. The argument would be big news, a fight would go viral.

"Bruh, just don't say shit to me again. Ever," Callie growled.

"Same here," Zenobia replied only to be defiant. Then turned to Lacrecia. "Oh, and I'm putting your shit out in the hall. Get it or don't."

❄

"MY FIRST SINGLE is gonna be

called, Fuck them bitches," Penny pondered as Malik played beats for her new solo project.

"Yeah, no, I don't think that's a good idea," he replied. He had actually seen this before a few times. Most groups breed stars and stars need their own room to shine.

"Had to drop that dead weight," she said, mainly to herself. Her fingers snapped when she liked the sound of it. "That's it, Dead Weight!"

"Less slanderous but better," the man sighed and labeled the track. He let it loop while Penny went into P-money mode and scribbled furiously on her pad. The title may have been a little less slanderous but the scathing lyrics were full of venom.

"I hate my job sometimes..." Malik sighed when P-money hit the booth and laid her feelings onto the thunderous beat. The catchy melody, infectious hook and subject matter meant another hit. It also meant the other thugs were going to have to clap back.

Penny made sure to post a few clips along with the hashtag 'deadweight'. It quickly went viral and added to the speculation about the group. People loved their music but they loved the drama even more.

CHAPTER 22

"I'm sorry ma'am, your card was declined," the waitress offered apologetically. She had run the card three times instead of the customary two just to be sure. Plus she was a fan and didn't want to fuck up her tip, autograph and possible picture with her favorite Pretty Thug.

"Huh?" Zenobia asked and squinted at her card to make sure it wasn't expired. She had just used it an hour before, buying clothes and baby supplies for Tiffany's son Mike junior. Her shoulders shrugged as she dug back in her Gucci purse and dug out another card. "Try this one."

"It must be they machine?" Tiffany guessed since she knew her friend had plenty of money. Zenobia shopped everyday but could afford it since her songs from both albums were still in heavy rotation on the radio.

"Must be!" she huffed in reply. The look on the waitresses' faces spelled more bad news before she reached the table.

"This one didn't work either," the girl pouted. "I can cover it with my tip money."

"The fuck wrong with my shit!" Zenobia asked and inspected this card as well as she could tell by looking at it. She couldn't so she shook it off and dug out some cash. She made sure to keep a few thousand dollars in cash with her at most times. Mainly because the dope man didn't take a Visa. "No sweetie. Thank you. Keep the change."

"Thank you!" the waitress cheered at the two hundred dollar bills to cover the fifty dollar lunch tab. It was plenty but she needed a little more. "Can I take a pic with you?"

"Sure. And I'm finna post it to my page," Zenobia sang and did just that. She made sure to tag the girl and tell her fans in the city to stop by and check her out.

"Bet you finna go to the bank and let they ass have it!" Tiffany exclaimed when they made it out to her car.

"In the morning. Ion feel like dealing with that shit right now," she replied since she always procrastinated when it came to her business. They chatted it up as she drove her over to her new apartment and helped her upstairs with all the etceteras babies require.

"Thanks again girl. I'ma pay you back one day," Tiffany vowed and blinked back the tears. Mike had run her through the wringer and left her high and dry. Her lifestyle had burned a few bridges with her family. The so-called group turned their backs on her as well. Zenobia was the only friend she had.

"I know," she sighed and turned to leave. Like most females she still followed other females she didn't like so she pulled up Callie's social page. She had just posted from the studio a few minutes earlier where she was hard at work on her new album. To add insult to injury she had reportedly turned down another five million dollar deal to stay independent.

"These hoes ain't worth a fuck," she spat, and checked Penny's page next. Every post had the same 'deadweight' hashtag. She tuned in to her live and listened to her pop shit to her P-hive. She arrived at her condo building to a flurry of activity. A sheriff, tow truck and pack of paparazzi were waiting on someone. "What now?"

"There she is!" a reporter announced and set off a frenzy towards her car. Zenobia had been getting a rash of interview requests about the Pretty Thug break up. She had nothing to say so she mashed on the gas and sped to her spot.

"Excuse me, Miss Lowe," A suited man called as he caught up with the sheriff at his side.

"She ain't home. I'll tell her you called," she said as she kept walking. Something she said a lot of lately since she didn't pay her bills like she should have. It wasn't for lack of money, some people just aren't good about handling grown up business. She was some people.

"Um, you're kinda a celebrity, so I can recognize you," the man replied while the deputy nodded.

"C-money," the officer and busted a half second Money Dance. "My daughter loves you."

"Well, let me sign a couple autographs for y'all so I can get some rest," she offered and went for her Sharpie. She had to be careful since she had coke and pills in her billfold.

"No ma'am. I'm with the IRS," he said and produced his credentials as well as her paperwork.

"Oh, ok. I got y'all letters upstairs. I'll uh, send a check?" she had to ask since she never opened any of the letters.

"No ma'am," he said apologetically since he disliked this

part of his job. "These are seizure orders. For the condo-minium. Mercedes Benz. Bank accounts..."

"So, y'all really finna take all my shit?" she snapped.

"Unless you can satisfy the tax debt by the court date," he explained hopefully.

"Is there anything you need to get from your car?" the deputy asked as a way of telling her that's why the tow truck was here.

"Naw man," she pouted and moped. She could only cry as her car was towed away. The blank space it left gave her a clear view of Penny's shiny Rolls Royce. At least they didn't take her phone so she summoned an Uber. Except the app couldn't run the card on file since her account was frozen. "Awe man!"

"DEAD WEIGHT HUH?" Callie chuckled as she entered the studio.

"Yeah but..." Malik said and shook his head. He knew if she clapped back it would just perpetuate itself. He could count on two hands how many rappers he recorded in this studio who are now on murals and t-shirts. Including Young Vaughn, Lil Bruh and Ethan. He couldn't help wondering how this new beef would play out.

"Ain't no but. This wigga, wannabe, pyromaniac, porn star..." Callie rambled a slew of slanderous slights for a full minute. "Want beef with me? I'ma a whole butcher out this bitch!"

"Yeah," he sighed and pulled up the beats. Her head bobbed to most of them for the next hour. She tagged a few for other songs but nothing fit the murderous mood she was in.

"That's it!" Callie shouted and jumped to her feet. She jumped, spun around, then literally ran into the booth.

"Here we go..." Malik sighed and hit record. Callie had written a few lines but most came straight from the heart and off the top of the dome. The man winced as the vicious one liners that took Penny apart like only someone who was once close can do. She laid her inner secrets and hidden fears all over the track.

The lyrics were bad but the hook was worse. The name of the song was Wigga Pleeze so she repeated it on the hook. She had a lot on her mind so she went for seconds on the second verse. This time she set her sights on Zenobia. Nothing was off limits including her father killing her mother, her drug use and now her financial problems.

"Oh my!" Dominique reeled as she caught the tail end when she entered the studio. Her eyes went even wider when they took it from the top so Callie could stack her vocals and add some adlibs. Callie went so hard she was literally out of breath by the time she left the booth. "That's how you feel?"

"That's how I feel," she confirmed with a shrug.

"Then that's what it is," Dominique confirmed. "We need to mash the gas on this. We can't let Penny beat us to market."

"How many songs she got done?" Callie asked. Dominique shrugged since she didn't know. They both knew who would know and turned to him.

"Wigga Pleeze!" Malik laughed since he wasn't telling them anything. He knew Penny had ten songs done to

Callie's four. The man had probably turned down millions in bribes for sneak peaks and leaks. Integrity is worth more than money so he was way ahead of the game.

The difference was P-money didn't need to put a lot of thought into her rhymes. Every song was about partying, shopping or balling. Callie on the other hand had something to prove. She wanted to be regarded as a serious lyricist. Not to mention Lecrecia's words rang in her head daily. The music turned her out. She had a responsibility to the young girls looking up to her. A responsibility she reflected in each song

"FIVE HUNDRED GRAND ain't gonna fix shit," Zenobia reminded herself. Tiffany jumped at the chance to put her up while she worked out her problems. She owed just north of two million in taxes so the advance from Jovita wouldn't make a dent towards settling the debt. Even with the million in her account. She would lose her condo and her car and be dead broke.

Doing shows wasn't an option since the group had broken up. Her sponsorship payments had dried up since she got dropped from most. Either for not fulfilling her quota of post, wearing other brands and most recently the bad publicity surrounding Flash's death.

"Fuck it," she said and accepted her losses. She came from the mud and could go back if need be. Ultimately she would be OK after her assets were sold to pay her debts. The royalties from sales, streaming and radio would provide a nice life.

"Don't say that!" Tiffany pouted. She didn't like seeing the woman she looked up to giving up. She rocked her baby and told him, "Tell yo auntie Z not to give up."

"I'm not giving up! I'm just accepting what it is!" she shot back. The doorbell rang and surprised them both. Each looked to the other to see who was expecting company.

"Don't nobody I know, know I stay here," Tiffany revealed.

"Me neither," Zenobia said. She didn't have a baby on her lap though so she got up to answer the door. At least she could take her frustrations out on whoever had the wrong door. She snatched the door open to read them their rights. A loud gasp escaped her throat when she saw who was standing there.

"What!" Tiffany reeled when Zenobia stumbled away from the door with a look of sheer terror on her face. The same look she had on her face when she saw her baby daddy standing there. She wanted to run but the fear had her frozen in place. Not that it mattered because Mike wasn't here to see her or their baby. In fact he never even looked over at them.

"I heard about your problems. I can help," he offered. He sounded sincere, except he still hadn't acknowledged his son a few feet away. His eyes never budged even when Tiffany found the courage to move. She eased down the hall and into her room.

"Help me?" Zenobia fussed but not cursing him out and telling him to beat it, left the door wide open.

"Yes. I know your label doesn't view you like they do the other girls," he laid out like a welcome mat.

"Hell naw!" she shot back and rolled her eyes.

"I do. I wanna sign you!" he said excitedly.

"OK so, you view me like the other two?" she asked and waited for his head to nod. "So give me five mil for my solo joint!"

"OK," Mike quickly replied with a shrug like money ain't a thang. Even if he did pay it, he would definitely recoup it and then some. Her hype alone was worth five million. Plus, Mike didn't necessarily have a positive image to uphold.

"Nuh-uh!" she dared and cocked her head dubiously.

"Un-huh!" he shot back while the wheels turned in his head on how to beat her out of it. "OK, your tax bill is two million. I got that for you. And, another million in your account. And another million once the album is done!"

"And? You missing a mil my nigga." she informed.

"OK, so four million then. Here's the first..." he said and placed a check on the table. Her hand moved toward it before her brain gave it permission.

"And I write my own lyrics! And wear what I wanna wear!" she insisted and pulled her hand back.

"Lyrics, sure. Wardrobe is on me," he said and licked his lips as he looked her over. He had a vision for this fine, yellow girl.

"No girl. Don't do it," Tiffany said to herself as she listened from through her door.

"Ummmm..." Zenobia hummed as she contemplated her future. The door had closed behind him when he left.

"I know you ain't finna do nothing with that nigga!" Tiffany exclaimed after Mike had been gone for several minutes. "He still ain't paid me what he was supposed to even with that flaw ass contract!"

"Huh?" she asked since she sure was thinking about it.

CHAPTER 23

"Is this bitch crazy?" Dominique asked as they watched Mike and Zenobia announce their new partnership.

"Yeah, high too I'm sure," Callie replied and nodded. She was right about Zenobia's being high. The first thing she did when she got back into her condo was snort, drink and smoke the night away.

"This other one might be high too," Dominique guessed when P-money followed up Mike and Zenobia on the music tabloid show. They were begging Callie for an interview but she wanted to let her music talk for her.

"Nah, that bitch just crazy," she laughed. A slight smile lifted a corner of her mouth since she kinda missed her crazy.

Her mind slipped away to the three broken girls in that dorm room. They were now rich and famous but she wondered if they were still broken. Her head shook when she decided she was fixed now. She wasn't one of them 'Ion need no man' chicks because Ervin made her whole. Just like Adam wasn't whole until he had his Eve.

"Yeah, that dis song is fucking crazy!" Dominique growled. Her contact at the radio gave her a heads up that it would be playing soon. Dead Weight was the first single off the album entitled, Dead weight.

"So is mine," Callie reminded since she had a scathing reply of her own. Even she would admit she went too far. Too deep and too personal.

"Knowing Mike, Z is going to record a response herself," her manager replied knowingly.

"I'm sure. Ion put nothing past her," Callie winced. There was just no telling what a high Zenobia was capable of. Even still, her next move would shock them all. Callie shook off the drama and got into Harlem mode before stepping into the booth. Malik cued up the next beat and she rode off to complete another song. Penny could be first to market but she wouldn't be far behind her.

Dominique began booking solo shows to spotlight songs from the new album. Callie still did her verses from the first two albums since they were in high demand.

"HEY," Mike greeted when he opened the door for Zenobia.

"We could have met at the studio!" she fussed since she was ready to get to work.

"We built a studio out back. We don't need our shit getting leaked," he explained as he led the way through his swank home.

Zenobia recalled the last time she had been here. Dominique was the queen of this castle since she was his woman. He usually kept a slew of young girls running around who would fuck on demand. Now it was empty and quiet except for the young man in the studio he had built in the pool house.

"Z this is Gilly. He's a producer/ engineer. Y'all gonna bang out some hits!" Mike cheered.

"Hey Gilly," Zenobia greeted with her good southern hospitality.

"Hey," he greeted stoically and didn't make eye contact. If she didn't know any better she would have assumed he was scared.

"Look, I know you wanted to write your own rhymes, but..." Mike began. He still had songs full of lyrics as licentious as the outfits he had for the luscious light skin girl. All her yellow lady curves would be on full display.

"And it's in our contract!" she reminded. High or not, she made sure to notate every detail she agreed to in the contract. It took three revisions since he kept 'forgetting' some of what they agreed upon. She even made him cut the IRS check before he got her signature on the line.

"A'ight. Just make it hot, like you," he demanded and sat. A nod at Gilly got him to preview the tracks they had for the project. Straight trap music, just like she liked it.

"Oh, it's finna be hot!" she assured and hugged her secret weapon. The book of rhymes and songs she inherited from the late, great, Young Vaughn.

"Well, I set a few things out for you. Let me know if you need anything. Food, drink, anything..." Mike offered and nodded. Zenobia followed his eyes over to a table with liquor, piles of weed and coke.

"Looks like we're good," she nodded. Her purse was packed with party favors but now she could save them for later. She waited until Mike left them alone before going over and digging in. She dove nose first into the coke and inhaled two lines up each nostril. "Have some?"

"God no!" Gilly grimaced at the thought of using the dangerous drug. He was from the hood too and saw the human tsunami of cocaine use and its aftermath. It amazed him that people actually still used it. It's not like the outcome is unknown.

"Shit, I'm feeling that!" Zenobia rocked and made fuck faces to the beat. It was hot, plus the rush of coke had her hyped.

"Spit something then!" Gilly dared.

"Say less!" she said and bounced into the booth. She flipped the rhyme book open and took off. Young Vaughn had taught her how to rap so spitting his words was like channeling his spirit. Now it was the engineers turn to twist his face up when she spit pure fire into the mic.

"The fuck!" Gilly grimaced again and bobbed his head along with her. He had heard her on Pretty Thug songs on the radio but didn't know she had this in her.

Zenobia ran through a complete song and hook within a few minutes. She fueled up on more coke and took a blunt back into the booth. Gilly pulled up a few more beats but she shook them off like a pitcher does the back catcher in baseball. She gave a thumbs up and nodded vigorously when she heard something she liked. She flipped to another song and went in once again.

"How's it coming?" Mike asked when he popped back in a few hours later. He knew she was the weak link out of the group so he didn't expect much.

"We knocked out four joints already big bruh!" Gilly exclaimed.

"Five!" she called back from the booth since they were working on the fifth. Gilly hit record and she laid down another song right before his eyes. He looked over and saw only residue of cocaine remained on the table. There was plenty more inside.

"Wow!" Mike clapped when she exited the booth. "At this rate we might just beat them to market!"

"We gonna beat them to everything!" Zenobia cheered and took a swig of her drink.

"Facts!" Mike agreed and excused Gilly. "See you tomorrow."

"Fa sho," the man agreed and slinked out of the studio.

"The designer dropped off a few outfits?" Mike asked since he didn't want to move too fast.

"Oh lawd!" she laughed. "Let me see."

"They're in the house," he said and led the way past the pool and back inside. They arrived in the den where more mounds of different drugs decorated the table.

"Y'all finna have me looking lil Lil Kim!" she laughed at the array of bikinis laid out on the pool table.

"You're gonna look way better than Lil Kim, Z-money, P-money, Beyonce..." he declared and watched her cheeks flush when she blushed. "Try one on?"

"Um, OK," she agreed and looked around.

"The bathroom is right there," he offered. Zenobia picked up a red one and rushed into the bathroom. Mike just chuckled at her attempt at privacy and pulled the camera feed from the bathroom up on his phone.

"Damn girl," he grimaced when she saw her yellow

curves. Her breasts looked bigger naked than clothed but that ass was as fat as expected.

"Issa lil small," Zenobia complained when she came out barely covered in the strips of red cloth. Hints of her brown nipples leaked from the top and mounds of yellow ass cheeks hung from the bottom.

"You prolly the baddest bitch I ever seen in my life," he stated as a matter of fact. It was true but he also wanted her to get accustomed to being called a bitch. Tiffany had filled her in on his foul temper and even fouler mouth but she was here anyway.

"Thank you!" she cooed and giggled at the perceived compliment. Only because she was still young, dumb and high. The word bitch negates whatever adjective comes before it and makes it an insult. But for some reason black folks reduced themselves to just niggas and bitches but swear black lives matter. How can they when bad bitch and real nigga are considered compliments.

"Have a drink!" Mike said urgently, before she could change back into her clothes.

"Um, OK," she agreed and joined him on the sofa. He watched her eyes go straight to the coke when she sipped her drink. His eyes dropped between her legs and wondered if she had an afro down there or if that pussy was really that fat. Little did he know that was all her. Her pussy lips were fatter than JJ Evans lips and it was dynamite.

"Hmp," he offered after lighting a blunt and taking a deep pull. She eagerly accepted it and took a few pulls herself. All the while eyeing the coke. "Have some..."

"Um, OK," she agreed and leaned in to inhale a few lines. Mike pushed his luck and fondled her ass while she bent over. They shared a serious look that could go either way once she sat up. He was still feeling lucky so he leaned in for a kiss. Only halfway though so she had to join him in the middle. She did and his tongue slipped into her mouth.

"Mmmm," Zenobia moaned when he reached between her legs and palmed her pussy through the bikini bottom. Mike pushed the issue and laid her back. He popped a titty out of the top and devoured it, while fondling the other. Zenobia moaned loudly when he switched nipples. He kissed down her hard stomach and began to eat her through the bikini.

"Take them off!" she pleaded and bucked her hips.

"You do it," he said, to make her work for it. She snatched the bottom off like Superman does his clothes when he was ready for action. Zenobia was too and she was about to get it.

Mike scooped her legs on shoulders and plunged his tongue into her pussy. She hissed and grabbed the back of his head when she bust a nut in his mouth. His beard was glistening when he finally lifted his face. Zenobia was ready for the dick but he wasn't ready to give it to her yet. Instead he picked her up like a groom does a bride when crossing the threshold. Except he was just taking her upstairs to fuck the daylights out of her.

"OK yeah," Zenobia giggled when she saw the sex pillow on the bed. Tiffany had told her all about them. As bad as he treated her and as much as he stole from her, she still bragged on the dick.

So far he had kept his word. He paid the tax debt and cut a million dollar check. Thanks to Young Vaughn's rhyme book the album would be done in a week. Now it was time to see what the dick was talking about. Mike leaned over towards the dresser but didn't grab a condom. Instead he scooped a small amount of the beige powder into a nostril.

"A'ight now! Mess around and yo dick not gonna work!" she fussed. The late Pretty Boy never got a chance to hit since he was always coked up.

"This is boy," he laughed. She didn't understand but was about to find out heroin had the opposite effect. He flipped that fat, round, yellow ass over and propped it up on the pillow. Then literally fucked the daylights out of her.

CHAPTER 24

"Is this bitch crazy!" Dominique reeled and blinked at the image on the TV. There was Mike and Zenobia booed up in public as they announced the new album, Trap Queen. She took Penny's title as a dis and laid out a dis song in reply. Callie wasn't spared either since she came to Lecrecia's aid after her treachery. All the songs were laid and being mixed and mastered.

"Must be," Callie confirmed and shrugged. She was only concerned with her own album, Going Back to Callie. She had laid thirty five songs but planned to whittle it down to twenty five.

"You know what..." Dominique was saying. Her voice cracked from the emotions but she managed to move on. "What do you think about the show?"

"I'm with it!" she cheered. Not just because she was getting paid a hundred grand for the set. Performing her new album along with the other Thugs would show the world who the top Thug really was.

"Bet. Same stage, same time," she informed.

"As long as I ain't gotta do them wack ass songs from them albums!" Callie grimaced. She had trained herself to hate the old music even though they dropped new money into her accounts every month.

"Nope. Easy money," her manager said and called the promoter to confirm.

'GAWK, GAWK, GAWK,' Zenobia's throat croaked as she serviced her man as the new album played through the speakers. Gilly just looked straight ahead at the monitors.

"Fuck!" Mike shouted and gripped her head so she couldn't get away. Not that she really tried. Mike had saved her, kept her high and so far treated her nicely.

"Boo!" she protested once she lifted her head and wiped her mouth. She popped a quick kiss on his lips and scurried away from his grasp.

"Told you about that," he growled playfully and tried to grab her.

"Mmhm," she laughed and bobbed her head to her songs. Her ass couldn't help but bounce to the bass heavy trap music. Gilly turned his head for a split second before turning back to the monitors.

"Ass fat ain't it?" Mike asked with a laugh and stood.

"Nah, I just, I mean, it is, I was..." Gilly stammered. He had been warned not to even look at Zenobia so that glance was going to cost him. Mike reeled back and slapped a spark out of the man. The blow knocked him completely out of his chair.

"Un-uh! Don't do him like that!" Zenobia protested. Gilly was nice and never said anything out of the way while they worked over the last few weeks.

"Oh, you protecting him?" Mike asked with his head tilted sideways. Battered women know this as the Ike Turner posture.

"I..." she was saying until a slap knocked it back down her mouth. Zenobia landed right next to Gilly and looked up in shock. This was a pivotal moment in her life like so many women before her. The reaction to that first slap, punch or even verbal abuse is the catalyst. It will either be the first slap, or last slap.

If a woman calls the police, leaves and never comes back it could very well be the last slap. To forgive, forget, accept or overlook and it will definitely be the first of just many abuses and beatings to come.

"What the fuck!" Zenobia spat as she climbed back to her feet.

"You tell me! You fucking him? Everything I did for you and you riding for the next man!" he moaned in classic narcissistic fashion. Now he was the victim.

"No baby! I'm sorry for making you feel like that!" she apologized like he was one with a busted lip. Gilly just stayed down so he couldn't get knocked down again.

"Just like Dominique..." Mike sighed as she comforted him. He had already sold her on how terribly she treated him before she left him. Have him tell it, Dominique broke her own jaw.

"No baby! I'm so sorry," she pouted and pulled him towards the house to pacify him with some pussy. She was supposed to ask for the million she had coming for completing the album. It would have to wait for a while since he was so upset.

"I WANT DOUBLE WHATEVER THEY GET!" P-money insisted. She was feeling herself since her streams and followers were going through the roof since she leaked a snippet of the dis track.

"I'm not in a position to negotiate with the promoter. It's a take it or leave it kind of deal," Jovita explained.

She had her reservations about having all three on the same stage but it would be a huge promotional opportunity. P-money wasn't a lyricist like Callie but the album was hot. They would recoup that five million in a few months, then double, triple and quadruple it.

"Fine! I just want to stunt on these hoes! I..." Penny was saying but Jovita cut in on her.

"You, are tripping is what you are," Jovita cut in. She had been trying to hold her tongue but couldn't anymore. "I'm here for the competitive spirit. I get that, but you are friends!"

"We were! Until they, until she," Penny replied but couldn't remember why she was so mad at her former friends. It was the fame but she couldn't see it since it swallowed her up as well. "Whatever! They know what they did!"

"Well, it's good they know..." Jovita quipped, and moved on. "The album is dope! So dope, I personally don't think we need the dis track."

"Dead Weight? That's the title of the whole album!" Penny reeled. Mainly because her fans were gassing it up.

The hashtag 'dead weight' was trending worldwide. "And, I have total artistic control!"

"You do," the CEO nodded since it was in her contract. She just shrugged her shoulders and hired more security. This show was going to go crazy.

"BABE, since the album is done, can we handle the business now?" Zenobia asked as they rode in the limo to another packed arena. The combined album release party was in such demand it took the same place the Atlanta Hawks played to contain it.

"I just bought you a fucking Rolls!" he reminded. The new car was just delivered that morning but only cost half of the million he owed her. Plus it was in his name instead of hers.

"Oh yeah!" she giggled and let it go. She had every one of the million dollars he gave her in her bank account. Even though Mike was going to report the whole four million so she was liable for taxes on it. Which meant she was broke.

"Once you do a few songs I want you to swing on one of them," he said. He had thought about it and decided it wouldn't be a good look for her to get her ass whooped, so he specified. "The white girl. Swing on the white girl."

"I'm not finna fight nobody on no stage!" she shot back. Mike flinched and caused her to duck like battered women do when their batterer makes a sudden movement.

"Bitch you gonna do," he growled and grabbed her cheeks like a grandma does a bad ass grandchild. "Whatever the fuck, I say do!"

"OK!" relented and he released his grip. Luckily there wasn't enough time to get her ass whooped like she did at home. Gilly, who doubled as a driver, glanced up in the mirror then back to the road. He was glad Mike didn't see since he got his ass whooped too.

"Good! Save the dis song for last," Mike directed since Zenobia was scheduled to go first in the song rotation. Each former Thug got to perform ten songs off their new albums in a round Robin fashion. The promoter used their number of followers to determine the order. Zenobia was first, followed by Callie and last Penny.

"OK," she sighed. She and Callie both leaked lines from their dis songs after Penny leaked hers.

"Let Callie do hers. Then, when the white girl turn come, sock her ass right in her mouth!" he laughed at his sinister plan.

"OK," she agreed again and Gilly gave another peep through the mirror.

"The fuck!" Mike exclaimed when they reached the crowded arena. He saw a sea of girls of every color and hue decked out in P-money pink. They gave way to another flock in Z-money's yellow. Then Callie's favorite color, blue.

"We out here!" Zenobia nodded when she saw her city showed up and showed out. She stood through the open sunroof and hyped them up as they passed by. Gilly parked next to the other limos and came around to open the doors.

"A'ight now lil nigga," Mike warned as he stepped out. Gilly took that warning and turned his head nearly 180 degrees like the exorcist so he couldn't say he looked under Zenobia's tiny dress. Which made no sense at all since if a man ALLOWS his woman to come outside in skimpy, scanty clothing he can't get mad if someone looks.

Security let them inside the back entrance while the fans filed inside the main gates. The general admission for the large open area was a recipe for disaster. The extra security focussed on keeping the girls away from each other until they reached the stage.

"Z-money," the promoter cheered from in front of her dressing room. He pushed the door open to allow them entry and confirm her rider was correct.

"Nice," Mike said of the bottles of champagne and liquor. Buckets of crab and crab legs that would not be eaten since they were both too coked up to eat.

"Let me change..." Zenobia said and retrieved her yellow outfit for the night. The yellow laced bra and thong looked lovely but begged the question, "How am I supposed to fight in this?"

"Even better!" he laughed. Zenobia was his woman but he didn't mind the world seeing her ass as she fought on stage. Then, take her home and fuck her.

"ION KNOW why I gotta go second!" Callie fussed as she looked at the likes and comments on her last post. Dominique just waited and watched as she pulled up P-money's page. Her lips twisted when she saw she had a few million more followers.

"Don't really matter. You're gonna be the dopest thing on that stage!" her manager reminded her.

She was right too because Callie was as lyrical as Lauren

Hill, Jay-Z or anyone else. Zenobia was coming in a close second since she inherited a book of rhymes. It was enough songs for several more albums. P-money was ten percent lyrics and ninety percent hype.

"Yeah," Callie agreed and twisted her lips. Her body was here but her mind was a million miles away.

"What's wrong?" Dominique asked when she saw the woman go inside her own mind.

"Wrong? It's not wrong," she replied, smiled and placed a hand on her stomach.

"Oh hell naw! Callie! Are you serious!" she cheered at the news.

"Yup, just found out," she sighed.

"That's dope! What Ervin say?" Dominique asked and came over to touch her flat stomach.

"We are about to see. I'm going to tell him tonight," she said with a wicked grin. Ervin would be in the sky box so he would get the news along with the tens of thousands in attendance as well as the millions around the world. A knock on the dressing room door interrupted their revelry.

"Show time!"

CHAPTER 25

Z-money got her mic as she stepped from her dressing room. She was so high and so hyped she couldn't wait to even get on the stage. She didn't, and launched into an a capella that whipped her city into a frenzy. Penny and Callie may have been the bigger artists, but this was her city.

"Make some 'muhfuckin noise Atl!" she screamed when she finally reached the stage. The city responded and went wild.

"Look what he got this child wearing," Dominique said and shook her head. That was something she and Mike had butted heads about when they were still together. He had a low regard for women in general so he wanted to dress the girls like prostitutes.

"Why does she have so much damn makeup on for?" Callie wondered since she knew the yellow girl didn't like or need makeup.

"Because he's whooping her ass!" Dominique shot back since she knew all too well. Once upon a time Mike had her covering black eyes and hand marks. Callie let out a deep sigh as her heart broke for her once friend. She was so deep in her feelings she didn't even hear her name being called. "Callie! Get your head in the game!"

"Word!" she said and snapped out of it. She lifted her mic and jumped feet first into an intro she had written just for the occasion.

"The fuck is this goofy bitch smiling at!" Mike snarled when Zenobia smiled proudly at her friend's introduction.

The verse was hot and Zenobia couldn't help but smile and bob her head along with her. The two smiled at each other whether they liked it or not. Once the heart is involved it can override the head. Still, pride is a mother fucker so they couldn't hug. They both laughed and shook their heads as P-money made her appearance. She flew over the stage like Supergirl, then hovered and rapped in midair.

"If I ain't know no better..." Jovita joked as she joined Dominique side stage.

"I know right!" she agreed since they sure looked like the old group. Even if the crowd was divided. The audience was clearly battling each other to be the loudest in support of their Thug.

Mike was the only one who wasn't smiling. Instead he wore a scowl since he loved controversy. The drama he caused with his knockoff Pretty Thugs made him a very rich man. Now that he owned one of the original Pretty Thugs he planned to get even richer. He would definitely recoup the money he spent to purchase Zenobia just off her fan base. Her stock would rise after she beats up P-money for the world to see.

"Atl shit shawty!" Z-money shouted and took off. She

rapped and twerked while her fans went crazy. Her counterparts wondered if she wouldn't just show her up.

Penny would have preferred to do this in Iowa, or Idaho
where her P-hive was deeper. Even though plenty showed
up here for the event. Still she made the call like Trump did
on Jan 6th. Little white girls threw tantrums and threatened
to kill themselves if their parents didn't take them.

Callie could definitely relate after her solo show in
Madison Square Garden. She still found herself smiling and
rocking along with Zenobia's first song. Even if she was a
little embarrassed for her, by what she was wearing. P-money
was squeezed into a pink tube dress that showed off her lady
lumps as well. While Callie was subdued in a throwback
Mary J Blige outfit.

"OK then. I hear that!" Callie applauded when Z
wrapped up her first song. It was now her turn so she
jumped feet first into that Harlem shit. Callie's fans whipped
into a frenzy and cheered her on. She ripped through her
verse and bust a 'how you like me now' pose when she
finished.

"OK, then!" Penny cheered cordially. It was her turn now
and the P-hive went crazy.

The fans were the big winners since they got to see their
favorite Thugs perform their new songs. Some were calling
out for the dis songs, while others requested their favorite
songs from the first two albums. The girls continued on with
the new music. Mike counted down and smiled when they
reached the end of their set. Now it was time for the dis song
to set up the fight. When P-money tried to clap back she
would get slapped down.

"Yo Atlanta!" Callie shouted before her second to last

song. The time was right so she looked towards the sky box. "I just wanted to share the good news with you all and my man. We're pregnant!"

"Yoooo!" P-money cheered and hugged her old friend. They all

suddenly remembered where they came from and couldn't help but be proud of where they were going. Zenobia was supposed to spit her dis song but joined the kumbaya moment.

"No! No! Don't do it!" Mike yelled but couldn't be heard over the crowd noise. Zenobia joined the group hug against his will. The crowd may have loved the beef, but they still had hearts. Hearts like love and softened. Not Mike though, he didn't have one. "You're supposed to be swinging, not hugging!"

"Now, y'all wanna hear some of the old shit?" P-money dared and discarded the dis song that was next. The arena erupted when the Money Dance began thundering through the massive sound system. It was like old times when they launched into the song and dance that made them famous.

"I got a trick for your stupid ass!" Mike laughed, his sinister, black hearted ass laugh and set his plan into motion. A group text went out to the agent provocateurs he had scattered about the arena. They were spread among every group to get an even response.

"Fuck P-money!" a girl in a C-money shirt shouted and socked a white teen in her eye. Her mother protested and got socked too.

"Fuck you niggers!" White girl Ki-ki shouted and punched a black girl. Mike paid her a thousand dollars to do it but she got a five thousand dollar ass whooping. Not that he cared since he was only interested in the carnage he started.

A smile spread on his face as the chaos ensued. The whole arena went crazy as the different factions attacked each other. The P-hive all carried P-money patent pending pepper spray in their P-money purses. Security rushed from all directions to stop the fray but were grossly outnumbered.

"Y'all chill! Un-uh, don't do that! Stop it!" Callie, Zenobia and Penny all screamed through their microphones but the mob was too far gone.

"We have to go!" Jovita screamed when she saw the security running back the other way.

"Come on!" Dominique shouted as they ushered the girls off the stage. They all rushed for the back entrance to escape together. They could sort themselves out once they were safely away from the all out riot.

"Come on!" Mike growled and snatched Zenobia away. He carted her away like a sack of flour and tossed her into the back of their limo.

"We should help her!" Penny shouted but gun shots made them hit the deck. They hopped into Dominique's SUV when there was a break in gunshots.

"Hope she's OK," Callie said as they fled the parking lot. Penny was literally shaking from the close call, so her close friend hugged and held her. "We're good. She's good!"

'A RAP BATTLE turned deadly in Atlanta last night...' the reporter reported the next morning.

"Oh no!" Callie moaned and began to sob. They

managed to escape the chaotic scene that raged on for hours after it began. Mike started the riot for publicity but it spiraled out of control. Some people are just evil so they attacked anyone around them.

"I'm just glad you all got out of there!" Ervin sighed. He and several others got stuck in their sky boxes while the riot raged on below. It looked like a scene from the Purge. At one point he had to let people in to escape the violence.

"I'm glad you did! I was so worried about you!" she pouted and snuggled up against him.

"Uh, you left my ass!" he laughed and got a pop.

"Boy I called you and told you to stay put!" she reminded.

"You did. We need to go ahead and get married," he offered once again rather nonchalantly.

"That was so ho-hum!" Callie complained and popped him again.

"Compared to announcing our baby in front of millions!" he laughed. He knew she was right though so he stood, dug into his pocket and knelt. Callie saw the ring box and lost it.

"Yes! Yes! Hell yes!" she cheered, bounced and spun around.

"Bruh, I ain't even asked nothing yet," he reminded and shut her down. Once she became semi still he began to speak. "Now, would you do me the honor of becoming my...."

"Yes! Yes! Fuck yeah!" she shouted, snatched the ring and put it on her own finger. Ervin just shook his head and laughed. This was the same behavior he fell in love with so he knew what to expect.

Her phone had been buzzing since they began speaking so she finally stopped to take the call and spread the news. A smile lifted the corner of her mouth when she saw the picture of Penny with her eyes crossed on the screen. It had been her caller ID picture since they met. If something good came out of last night's conflict it was that some of the malice in their hearts dissipated.

"Hey girl! Guess who is getting married?" she dared. Penny didn't even hear the question though.

"It's uh, Zenobia," she croaked. "It's bad..."

"What's wrong!" Ervin asked when he saw the look on his fiance's face as she scrambled to get dressed.

"It's, Z,z,z, Zenobia. She might not make it!" she repeated and collapsed. Ervin sprang into action and helped her up, dress and straight to the hospital.

"HEY GIRL!" Jovita greeted as she and Dominique arrived at Grady hospital at the same time.

"Hey," Dominique replied and hugged her. The weariness was evident in her eyes and voice. Her doctor had been here all night dealing with the aftermath of the concert riot. They turned and headed into the hospital. The waiting room was jam packed but one face stood out through the crowd. "Grrrrr!"

"I'm going up," Jovita called after her as she marched over towards Mike.

"What did you do to her!" she demanded. Her eyes scanned the immediate area for something to bust him in his head with.

"Me?" he reeled and raised his hands in surrender. "I didn't do anything! She got caught up in that madness last night!"

"Bullshit!" Dominique barked. Most people may have bought his performance but she knew the man too well. Plus she knew they got the girl out of the venue. So whatever happened to her didn't happen in there.

"Ass still fat!" he called after her as she marched away.

"Zenobia Lowe?" Dominique demanded when she reached the ICU.

"Last room, on the right," the nurse reluctantly replied. The patient needed rest but she didn't feel like fighting the angry woman.

Dominique marched down the hall like a North Korean soldier. What she saw when she walked in made her knees buckle. A broken arm was suspended in a cast and her face was nearly unrecognizable. Zenobia's yellow skin was a rainbow of red, purple and black. Black stitches ran through her top lip.

"Her jaw is broken," Jovita informed and blinked. She kept blinking to remove the image of her shooting Mike in his face. Her gun was in the car so she blinked again.

"He did this," Dominique said and rubbed her own jaw.

"She can't have visitors!" Dominique's doctor boyfriend announced as he came into the room. If Jovita didn't know any better she would have assumed the two never met by his tone.

"Is she going to be OK?" Jovita needed to know before she could leave her.

"Eventually. Nothing is fatal. Broken bones, swelling on the brain, detached retina..." Carl laid out hotly.

"What's wrong babe?" Dominique had to ask on the way out of the room.

"Really!" he reeled, wide eyed as he pointed to the battered young woman on the bed.

"I didn't do it!" she shot back hotly.

"You may as well have. It's the business. Your business," he said and sighed. "I pronounced a twelve year old dead five minutes ago. A sixteen year old last night..."

"I'm so sorry baby!" Dominique moaned and wrapped him up to comfort him.

"You have to choose. Me or this!" he demanded and pulled away.

"You or my career?" she asked for clarity. His head nodded and forced her to decide on the spot.

CHAPTER 26

"There's Penny!" Callie said and reached over to honk the horn as Ervin drove to the hospital. She had to literally lean on it since Penny was too far into her head to hear the horn. It would have to wait until they both parked in the parking lot.

"Callie!" Penny shouted and ran over to slam into her. They almost went down from the impact but Ervin was close enough to hold them up.

"How is she?" Callie asked. She had been calling the hospital the whole way to the hospital but couldn't get any answers since no one answered the phone. They had their hands full with the mass casualty incident from the night before.

"Don't know," she replied and they turned to go inside and find out.

"What are they doing here!" a woman shouted as two of the three Thugs entered the waiting room.

"My baby fighting for her life 'cuz of y'all!" a white

woman shouted. She was followed by more shouts and boos until hospital security as well as Atlanta police had to escort them out of the hospital before they got attacked too.

"Let's get out of here!" Ervin urged and put them both into his car.

Jovita sat in her own car holding the pistol on her lap. Mike had no idea how close he came to death when he walked right by her. Seeing the mob practically chase the girls from the building snapped her from her murderous daze. She pulled her phone and called Penny, Callie, then Dominique.

"Meet me in the office!" she ordered everyone and hung up. She arrived first since everyone else procrastinated with their reservations. In the interim she followed the backlash against her girls. The media put the blame squarely on the Pretty Thugs. Four people had died and several more were fighting for their lives. Including Zenobia.

"Hey..." Dominique offered as she walked in. It was obvious she had more to say but she sighed and sat instead.

"Yeah," Jovita agreed. She had called this emergency meeting but still had no idea what it was about. She was the boss, so she was determined to fix it, if it could be fixed. They were both relieved to see Penny and Callie arrive together.

"Man this is all fucked up!" Callie lamented. She and Penny stayed right next to each other just like they did the first time they came here. Like scared young ladies leaning on each other for comfort.

"It is. And I'm not sure how to fix it," the boss sighed.

"Nothing to fix. I'm done," Callie said and looked down at the ring on her finger. Penny saw the ring and had a delayed reaction.

"Nuh-uh! Word? Dang!" Penny reeled, sounding like all three thugs in one.

"Yeah, he just asked me today," she said stoically. Dominique looked up as an idea came to mind, but she didn't share.

"Congrats chica," she said and managed a soft smile. This was Callie's moment so she held her tongue for now.

"Well, I guess my album should wait?" Penny wondered, then nodded along with her own assessment.

"We couldn't possibly release an album at a worse time!" Jovita admitted even though she was over six million dollars in on the project. There was too much backlash at the moment and it would be totally insensitive to the dead kids. "Speaking of insensitive..."

"Scrap it! Delete it..." Penny shot back since she knew exactly what she was talking about. She had already made up her mind not to include the dis song on the album when they were on stage together. She even deleted the snippet from her social media. Callie gave Dominique a nod that meant the same. There would be no dis songs on either of their albums.

"We have no control over Zenobia's project," Jovita reminded.

"Shit, neither does she!" Dominique shot back. She knew first hand Mike controlled her, everyone and everything around him with an iron fist. Even Gilly was sitting up in Grady hospital with a broken jaw of his own. He tried to intervene when Mike beat and stomped Zenobia for not performing the dis song or starting the fight onstage. Mike even made him drive themselves to the hospital after whooping their asses.

"Something has to be done about him," Jovita sighed. She had let him walk right by her car with her gun on her lap. She may have killed someone, but she was no killer.

"It will be," Dominique said and glanced at Callie's wedding ring again. A slight smirk appeared on her face as she plotted. This was her chance to share so she did. "My man called himself giving me an ultimatum! Him or the music biz!"

"Whoa! Wow! Girl!" the three women reeled. Callie had to ask, "What did you say?"

"I chose him. I'm out," she informed to nods and smiles all around. She chose love and anyone can understand that.

'GAWK, GAWK, GAWK!' some nameless bird squawked each time Mike thrust into her larynx.

"Gilly!" he shouted when whoever was ringing the doorbell like crazy kept ringing the doorbell like crazy.

"Yeah boss?" he answered through the wires in his mouth and tried to ignore the girl he had picked up for Mike as he fucked her tonsils. Her eyes fluttered like she needed assistance but assistance got his ass whooped last time.

"Get the damn door!" he ordered as he stroked.

"Ok boss. I was in the bathroom," he explained as an excuse. He didn't even get to wipe good since Mike was screaming his name.

Gilly ran down the stairs and pulled the door open to find twelve of Atlanta's finest standing there with a warrant. He smiled as much as the wires would allow and ushered them inside.

"Soup's on!" Mike laughed to himself and flooded the girls mouth with millions of little mike and mike-ettes. His fun was interrupted when the cops rushed in to arrest him. "Fuck y'all doing!"

"You're under arrest for the assault on Zenobia Lowe," the lone detective said once the uniformed cops had him in cuffs. He looked at the naked girl on the bed and asked, "Are you OK?"

"Yes," she answered and grabbed her clothes. The detective cleared the room so she could dress, then questioned her again. She confirmed her consent to the sex act and verified her age. Gilly agreed to take her home once the cops took Mike to jail.

"That bitch really pressed charges on me?" Mike asked as he was booked into jail. He usually whooped asses so thoroughly no one ever pressed charges on him before. Zenobia had been discharged to recover at home a week later. Dominique told her about her plan and she smiled and nodded through her own broken jaw.

"Actually a witness did," the detective informed and showed him the statement. His eyes blinked Dominique's name into view and he couldn't believe his eyes. He was processed and immediately called for an attorney visit.

"Gilly came through!" he cheered as he entered the secure room to speak with his lawyer. He had called over his shoulder to call his lawyer as he was led away. Except, this wasn't his lawyer. "Who are you and what the fuck is she doing here?"

"I'm attorney William Edwards," he answered and turned to his guest to answer for herself.

"Believe it or not, I'm here to help you," Dominique said.

"Bitch you the one who pressed charges!" he reminded hotly.

"Nah, I'm the one who gave the statement. The state is pressing charges." she explained. "Now, when Z testifies against you, you're going to prison."

"If Miss Lowe declines to testify she will be held in contempt," the lawyer explained. "If you were legally married she cannot be compelled to testify against you."

"How much?" he turned to Dominique and asked. "How much do you bitches want?"

"She doesn't want a dime from you. She still loves your rotten ass for some reason. Go ahead and marry her and this goes away," she shrugged as if it were that simple.

"Do I look fucking stupid to you?" Mike asked but quickly realized he was setting himself for an insult. "Marry the bitch and she takes my shit in a divorce."

A nod from Dominique prompted the lawyer to go into his attaché case. He came out with a document and slid it across the table. They both watched Mike's eyes scan each line until he reached the bottom and looked up.

"So, let me get this straight..." he began and tilted his head like it was a dare. "She will sign a prenuptial agreement and not testify against me, if I marry her?"

"Yup. She loves you," Dominique replied. "I however hate your guts. So this intervention is gonna cost you."

"I would expect nothing less. We're just alike, me and her," he told the lawyer, then turned to her. "Just alike. From the Bricks. No one gave us shit, so we took. We're takers, that's what we do."

"Whatever, but it's gonna take five hundred to get me to recant and walk away," she reminded since her testimony matched Zenobia's injuries. That was more than enough to convict him with a jury.

"Dial 679-221..." he said until Gilly's phone rang and was answered.

"You good boss?" he asked.

"Gonna be. Go into the safe and pull out five hundred. Then..." he was saying before Gilly had a question.

"Five hundred dollars? I got that in my pocket," the man offered eagerly. He suffered from the same Stockholm syndrome many abuse sufferers suffer from.

"No you stupid muhfucka! Half a mil. Take it to..." Mike snapped then handed the phone to Dominique to tell him where to meet.

"I'll handle your bail once this is done," the lawyer said and stood. He extended his hand to be shook but Mike just glared at him. Then turned his vicious glare on Dominique until they cleared the room.

"ON GOD, this is the craziest shit I've ever seen in my life!" Callie protested. She bought her dress and flew to Jamaica for the private wedding but didn't agree with it one bit.

"But, I love him," Zenobia moaned.

"I'm sorry, I can't understand you with your jaw wired shut!" Penny snapped for the same reason. Mike had released her album including the dis song but she got past that. It was these nuptials that pissed her off.

"I know," Zenobia pouted and threatened to cry, which would mess up her makeup.

"This is what she wants. We have to support her!"

Dominique urged and calmed the rest. She had been the only one in support of this madness.

"I guess," Jovita said and twisted her lips.

The ceremony was supposed to be low key but the three Pretty Thugs were spotted and word got out. The group wanted to stay out of the spotlight for a while after the deadly concert. News of the union quickly spread around the globe.

"I just want to be a wife," Zenobia admitted. Lots of women do and never get to. Most are smart enough not to marry a man who is definitely going to whoop their ass though.

"Shoot me and Ervin should go on and tie the knot while we're down here?" Callie wondered out loud. Her friends couldn't answer so she would wait and ask him once the wedding was over.

"Well, you look beautiful!" Jovita gushed and snapped another picture.

"I hope he thinks so," Zenobia said since she and Mike hadn't seen each other since he put her in the hospital. Dominique had handled all arrangements to make this happen.

"It's time mon," a worker announced. They followed him out to the veranda on the beach where Mike was waiting. Gilly was by his side as his best man since he didn't have any actual friends. That's the thing about having friends. You have to be one, to have one. Anything less and it's just some mufuckas around each other.

"Hey there! You look beautiful!" Mike greeted and reached for her hand. Zenobia flinched from the movement like abused women will do.

"Un-uh," Ervin said and held Callie back. Seeing her friend flinch broke her heart. Zenobia was once as fearless as she was, now she cowered under some dude.

"I can't," Penny said for the same reason and walked off through the sand. She tried, but ultimately couldn't watch.

"You good?" Mike wanted to know. Broken jaw or no broken jaw he still wanted to fuck her on their wedding night.

"Huh? No, I mean yes. I mean, I'm gonna need a little time to get myself together," she explained as the preacher looked on curiously. He had performed plenty of marriages on this beach but none as odd as this. He got paid though so he shrugged his shoulders and proceeded.

"Shall we proceed?" he asked him and he looked at her.

"I'm on my cycle anyway. Time I come off, I'll be good," Zenobia nodded and agreed. Mike nodded but looked around for that pretty black chick who flirted with him right before the wedding. He took her number despite being here to get married. Someone was getting fucked on his wedding night.

They exchanged their 'I Dos' and rings but Zenobia flinched again when it came time to kiss the bride. She went stiff as a board as she offered her cheek. Mike kissed her cheek and spotted the chick he was looking for. She seemed unfazed by his nuptials so he winked. She winked back and it was a date.

"So I'ma see you later then," Mike offered and stepped away as her friends came to congratulate her. Except for Penny who was chatting it up with a regular guy she met in the hotel.

"O..." Zenobia was saying but he was gone before she could reach the k in OK.

"Hey! Hold up," Mike called as he followed the woman down the darkened beach.

"Catch up..." she laughed and walked even faster. He didn't have to run since she dipped under the cabana tent she had set up already to enjoy the ocean breeze while she worked.

"OK then..." Mike nodded at the setup. A blanket was spread on the sand along with her cooler and laptop.

"Congratulations!" she reminded when he looked her up and down. His eyes got stuck between her legs on her bikini bottom.

"Just for show," he said and moved on her. She put up no resistance when he scooped her up and put his tongue in her mouth. She gripped his dick through the linen shorts until she had a full fledged erection in hand. "Suck it for me..."

"Not on your wedding night Mr," she laughed as they laid down. She produced a condom from under the pillow and rolled it down his thick dick.

"I see you're prepared?" he asked assuming she was a working girl.

"Of course! This is my job," she said and proved him right. Not that he minded buying pussy in the least. Even on his wedding night.

The woman mounted him and worked the dick inside of her. She was good and wet from anticipation of what was to come. The good, stiff dick up inside of her was just gravy on the steak. She rocked, bounced and shimmied until she busted a good nut.

"Mmhm, I should get a discount!" Mike laughed as he flipped them both over so she was on her back.

"I can dig it," she laughed and pulled her legs back so he could dig her out. He did just that too until she came again just before he did. Mike pushed down to the bottom of her box and tested the strength of the condom.

"Mmp, shit, fuck!" he grunted and groaned as he skeeted into the latex. There were a few more positions he wanted to put her in but needed a bed for that. "Let's take it to my suite. What I owe you?"

"You already paid me Mike," she giggled and passed him a folded hundred dollar bill. "You snort boy?"

"I do," he said and happily took it. He didn't dare bring his own heroin on the flight since the stakes were too high. He had just reached the second nostril when he caught a couple of inconsistencies. First, her using his name when he hadn't given it. Second was, "And just how much did I pay you?"

"Half a mil. Thank you very much," she laughed as the drugs began to pull his head down to his chest.

She worked quickly to put his hands on the computer and wine bottle before she left. The deadly fentanyl dragged him towards death while she cleaned the crime scene. The condom was full of his DNA but it was hers on the outside. The cooler contained enough cleaning supplies to fix that problem. It also held a pistol in case he declined the drugs, Either way he was dying tonight. He was just another rich music exec who OD'd by the time she rushed away.

"The fuck?" Penny wondered when the woman rushed by with her head down while sending a text.

"What's wrong?" Callie asked when Penny came into the dining area looking perplexed.

"I could have sworn I just saw that chick Alizae?" she wondered and nodded with her own assessment.

"Who? Huh? Nah!" Dominique asked and answered quickly. A little too quickly for Callie's comfort. She looked over to the new bride who finally smiled for the first time on her own wedding night.

"Mmhm," Callie hummed. Her suspicions would be confirmed when the body of the music mogul was found in the morning. That was the end of Mike, and the end of the Pretty Thugs series...

THE END

EPILOGUE
THE AFTERMATH

The prenup spared Mike in a divorce but not from inheritance. Zenobia wasn't the only beneficiary of Mike's timely death. Tiffany's son was his only other heir so Zenobia cut the child into the inheritance. Zenobia split the assets with the kid, which gave Tiffany plenty to live off.

She recovered the stolen rights to all the music and returned them to their rightful owners. Which meant the Real Pretty Thugs as well as Lil Bruh's family would finally see some money off their efforts. White girl Ki-ki was able to stop flipping burgers and bought a double wide trailer. Jersey girl went back to Jersey and smoked every penny she received.

The house went to Mike junior since Zenobia's album did numbers. Even after she pulled the dis track. Her spitting Young Vaughn's lyrics proved to be a winning combination. One that his mother benefited from as well since she cut the woman in as well. The rhyme book contained enough songs for years to come.

Money can ruin plenty of people but Zenobia wasn't none of those people. The more she got, the more she gave. To everyone except Lacrecia that is. That was a disrespect beyond return so she never spoke with her ever again in life. She actually forgave the girl but that doesn't mean having to fuck with her.

Lacrecia was good though since she birthed a baby boy for Flash. It took some legal haggling including lawsuits and DNA tests but she eventually got cut into his inheritance as well. She eventually shook off the street life and went back to school to become a doctor.

Jovita waited a full year before releasing Penny's album. The world has a short memory so it quickly shot to number one and produced a slew of number one hits. The best news came when the same detective from Vegas reached out with wonderful news.

Misty was found dead of a fentanyl overdose herself. Seems she was hanging out with some black chick from New York when she inhaled the deadly drug. There was some grainy security footage but Penny didn't identify the woman. Alizae made another half a million for a few of her services. Ironically Misty had no family so Penny was able to recover what was left of her late father's assets.

More good news came from across the world. Death Trap got cancelled for fucking with little girls. He avoided a bunch of rape charges by moving around non extradition countries. Where he fucked up was importing drugs for his new business as a drug dealer. He spread enough around to cause a problem. He was arrested and sentenced to the death penalty. Of course he now tried to get help from America but the embassy said, nah and let him die.

Callie eventually released her album independently but it didn't do much by sales. The lyrics were too positive and negative mufuckas don't like that. Even radio prefered bullshit they had to beep, than the uplifting songs. She did manage break even on what she spent but it didn't matter much to her since she andErvin had opened four more dealerships.

Her biggest flex was the small army of children she and her husband would go on to have. The girl who grew up lonely and alone would go on to have a huge family of her own. She had never been much for prayers but knew she failed miserably on her own. God gave her this so she thanked Him every day.

Dominique married her doctor and started a new career mentoring young girls. She walked away from the music business and never looked back. She used her ongoing commissions to fund her nonprofit organisation. The chick from the Bricks had finally found some happiness of her own.

Alizae retired from hitting licks and tried to live happily ever after. She tried to redeem herself by paying Brandon's way through college and law school. Except she had done to much dirt to get away Scott free. A brother of one of her victims caught up with her and choked her to death.

Jovita grew the company to one of the largest labels in the country. She was still looking for love but the billion in her bank account made up for it. She was hinting at a Pretty Thugs reunion tour one day but...